Ralph Dutton

Woman's temptation

A Novel. Vol. 3

Ralph Dutton

Woman's temptation
A Novel. Vol. 3

ISBN/EAN: 9783337273552

Printed in Europe, USA, Canada, Australia, Japan

Cover: Foto ©Andreas Hilbeck / pixelio.de

More available books at **www.hansebooks.com**

WOMAN'S TEMPTATION.

A NOVEL.

EDITED BY

THE HON. MRS RALPH DUTTON.

Such is my name, and such my tale,
Confessor—To thy secret ear
I breathe the sorrows I bewail,
And thank thee for the generous tear.

IN THREE VOLUMES.

VOL. III.

LONDON:
HURST AND BLACKETT, PUBLISHERS,
SUCCESSORS TO HENRY COLBURN,
13, GREAT MARLBOROUGH STREET.
1860.

WOMAN'S TEMPTATION.

CHAPTER I.

Ah! that deceit should steal such gentle shape,
And with a virtuous vizor hide deep vice.
                                        SHAKSPEARE.

THE next two or three days passed pleasantly enough, in curling, skating, sledging, and
any other amusements that the weather per-
mitted. All the ladies joined in them, except
Leonie, who was obliged to confine herself to
looking at the others, and being driven in a
sledge by all the gentlemen in turn. Lady
Arabella Burleigh and her sister, and Mrs
Tredegar, particularly distinguished themselves

among the ladies, and Leonie and Gertrude
sometimes sat for hours in their sledge, watching their feats of agility. Very often the party
would come out at five, well provided with
torches, and skate till it was time to dress for
the eight o'clock dinner. On one of these
occasions, little Lady Amy St Aubyn, catching
her foot on a rough piece of ice, as she was
flying after Sir Henry, was thrown violently
down, cutting her forehead, and bruising her
right shoulder severely. Everybody hurried
to her assistance, and Gertrude had her put
into her sledge, and took her home at once.
Her hurts were not found to be serious, but
she was much shaken, and as her shoulder required constant fomenting she was obliged to
keep her room for the rest of the evening.
Leonie, who had been somewhat tired with her
day's amusement, and was pleased with the
little creature's patience and fortitude, volun-
teered to stay with her and take care of her, an
offer which, after a little demur, was gratefully
accepted by Lady Amy.

After dinner they were visited by Lady Arabella Burleigh, who came in with a great deal

of flounce and streamer, kissed her sister, pushed her hair off her forehead—Lady Amy, rather pettishly, immediately pulled it back,—said, "Dear me! it was such a pity! so kind of Lady Bournemouth! she wished she could be of any use, but she was the most helpless person in a sick room," and then went down to say that there was not much the matter with Amy, but, dear child, she liked a little petting, and perhaps it was just as well to keep quiet, and really Lady Bournemouth was so kind—at all of which Lord Bournemouth looked much amused. Mr Burleigh was uneasy, said he was sure Amy wouldn't complain for a trifle, went up to Lord Bournemouth and thanked him in very warm terms for the care Lady Bournemouth was taking of his sister-in-law; adding that Arabella was the worst person in the world to apply to in case of illness, and would really be of no use, even if she did take Lady Bournemouth's place.

Meanwhile Leonie and her patient were very well pleased with one another, and as Lady Amy's shoulder became easier, and she

had been fortified by dinner, she became extremely lively and chatty, and the two were in
the midst of a very animated discussion, when
the door opened, and Gertrude came in.

"Leonie ! I want you ! come to my room,"
she said.

"I hope nothing has happened?" said Lady
Amy, alarmed.

"No—nothing ; I have something to say
to Leonie—that is all."

Leonie, however, saw that something had
happened, and followed her in great curiosity.
No sooner had Gertrude reached her room,
than she locked the door, threw herself into an
arm-chair, and began talking very quickly and
incoherently, and in such an agitated voice
that Leonie could scarcely make out what she
said.

"They were talking about jewels," she began, "Mr Elston and Mr Grant's second son,
who has just returned from India. They went
on from one thing to another till they began
about diamonds, and the different ways of
cutting and setting them, and Henry thought

my diamonds were set like that, and told me to fetch them. What shall I do?"

"Take them down," said Leonie, with a half suspicion of the truth.

"They are not here, Leonie!" shrieked Gertrude, springing up, and pacing up and down the room. "They are pawned! those in my jewel box are paste!" and covering her face with her hands, she burst into a torrent of tears.

"I suspected this," said Leonie, "when I found they would not cut."

"What am I to do? What shall I do? Oh, think of something, my head is in a whirl. Henry will be furious! and all these people! If I could only put it off till to-morrow!"

Leonie considered. "You can't do that. Sir Henry will see by your looks that something is wrong. Send for him here, and tell him all."

"Leonie! what are you thinking of? I can't—I can't—and every one will suspect. If it were only Mr Elston, I would take them down, and trust to his not finding out the difference; but Mr Charles Grant knows all about stones, and could tell directly that they are not real. I wonder if he would say anything about it?"

"And if he did not, would you throw yourself on the mercy of a stranger, rather than on that of your own husband? For shame, Gertrude! Sir Henry has not deserved this."

"That is just it," said Gertrude. "He has been so kind about paying my debts, and then to find that I have done this! Oh, I wish I were dead!"

"I don't think you are particularly fit to die just at present," said Leonie dryly. "My dear Gertrude, send for Sir Henry, and have it over at once. You will be far happier when he knows all. You can't have had any peace, with this on your mind."

"Peace! I have not known what it meant, ever since I did it. I have scarcely been able to keep up appearances, and go on receiving people. Oh, what shall I do!"

"Come," said Leonie, "take my advice, and send for Sir Henry. Depend upon it, it will be far better in the end. What message will you send him?"

"Whatever you like," said Gertrude, in an extinguished voice.

Leonie considered for a few moments, rang the bell, and desired that Sir Henry might be told Lady Kincardine wished to speak to him.

Gertrude turned deadly pale, as she heard the message given, and sprang forwards to stop the lady's-maid, but Leonie prevented her. She then sunk back into her chair, and covered her face with her hands, and Leonie observed that when Sir Henry's step was heard approaching she trembled violently.

"I will go now, Gertrude," she said.

"No! no! stay, I beg you!" exclaimed Gertrude, with such fear and agony in her tone, that Leonie hesitated; and before she had time to remonstrate, Sir Henry entered.

"Gertrude!" he said, "what do you want? What is the matter? Are you ill?"

Gertrude tried to speak, but her voice died away in sobs, and she motioned with her hand to Leonie.

It was decidedly more than Leonie had counted upon, to have to break the intelligence to Sir Henry; but there was no help for it, so she began, " You told Gertrude to bring down her diamonds;—but the fact is, she is in diffi- culties about her money affairs, and not liking to apply to you to settle them after you had paid so much for her, she very foolishly and wrongly pawned them."

The expression of surprise on Sir Henry's face died away, and was succeeded by one of great wrath.

" Gertrude!" he said sternly, in a tone of extreme displeasure; " I knew you were extra- vagant, but I never expected that you would be dishonest."

There was no answer, but Gertrude, turn- ing away from him, hid her face on the arm of the chair, while her whole frame was shaken with convulsive sobs.

" When did this happen ? " said Sir Henry shortly.

" Before she left London, I suppose," said Leonie.

" What sum did she receive for them ? "

" Gertrude !" said Leonie, "what was it ? "

" Three thousand pounds," murmured Gertrude.

" Is it all spent ? "

" All."

" Where are they ? "

" At Holme and Wilson's."

" Good; when all these people are gone, I shall go up to Town and get them."

Gertrude and Leonie both felt that this coolness was far more fearful than open anger. In fact, Sir Henry, the very soul of honour and straight-forwardness himself, was deeply hurt at his wife's deceit; which was aggravated by the fact that the diamonds were family ones, therefore not her own to dispose of. The thing seemed to him too monstrous for indignation, his grief defied words; nor would he have sought to find them, accustomed as he was to restrain his feelings.

" I meant to redeem them; indeed I did!" said Gertrude.

" With your extravagant habits, you know that would have been impossible," said Sir Henry, coldly.

" I would have done it, if I had sold all my own jewels! I will sell them now—I will do anything, if you will only forgive me! Oh, Henry, say you don't hate me!"

" I forgive you, Gertrude," he said in a repressed tone, as if he were suffering extreme pain, "though you have betrayed my confidence."

" Oh, Henry! dear Henry!" exclaimed Gertrude, "you hate me—I know you hate me!"

She felt as if she had never prized his affection so much as now, when she seemed likely to lose it, and her tone of misery touched him.

" I do not hate you, Gertrude," he said, " you very well know that it is scarcely in your power to shake my affection for you. I am quite ready to believe that you meant to redeem them. Whether you were right in pawning property that was not your own, or in conccaling such serious embarrassments from me, is a question you must decide for yourself."

" Indeed I never saw it in this light before!

I could not bear to apply to you after all you had paid for me, and so I did it without thinking whether it was right or wrong."

"Your own conscience must have told you that it was wrong, or you would never have concealed it from me," said Sir Henry, with a curl of his lip. "But let us have an end of this. I don't want to be hard upon you—you are very young and very thoughtless, and I can easily believe that in your difficulties you never stopped to reason the matter closely. But I must confess that I am deeply grieved at your want of confidence. Dearly as I love you, Gertrude, you might have trusted to my love!"

Gertrude sprang up, threw herself into his arms, and buried her face on his shoulder.

"Do you still love me? You will not give me up?" she whispered in suffocating sobs, and clinging to him as if she feared that he would at once shake her off, and leave her. "I shall never rest till I have regained your esteem—I will sell my jewels—I will retrench till I have paid every farthing of the money!"

"That is impossible, Gertrude," said Sir

Henry; "but we will not go into particulars
at present. To-morrow I shall expect you to
give me an account of how these debts were
made. We cannot stay any longer now—
every one will wonder what has become of us."

"I can't go down!" said Gertrude; "you
must make some excuse for me. Every one
will see that something has happened."

"You must," said Sir Henry, shortly, " or
we shall have the whole country-side gossip-
ing. I will go first, and say that the diamonds
are not set in the way I supposed, therefore
there would be no use in looking at them.
You can stay here till your eyes are fit to be
seen, and then, if you go to see Lady Amy
before you come down, no one need know how
long you have been with her."

Saying this in a very decided tone, he gently
replaced Gertrude in her chair, and left the
room, much to Leonie's relief, who had felt
herself to be decidedly in the way, and yet
could not find an opportunity of going.

"Thank Heaven that he knows it all,"
were Gertrude's first words. " Dear Leonie,
I can never thank you enough!"

"I hope, Gertrude, you will be more careful in future," said Leonie, anxiously. "Do let your retrenching be in earnest this time."

"How can it be anything else, after this dreadful business? And to-morrow I must show Henry all those horrible accounts!"

"Have you any?" said Leonie, in surprise.

"I have the bills—most of them, at least; and I know what I have done with the rest, within a few pounds."

"Well, that is better than I could have hoped. Now, have you washed your eyes? That is right—you are almost presentable, and will soon look very well."

"Oh, Leonie! I dread going down! I can never get through the evening!"

She looked so ill and wretched, that Leonie saw at once how unfit she was to return to the drawing-room.

"Suppose you go to Amy," she said, "and I down-stairs, and say you have taken my place for a short time?"

"Oh, that will just do;—but no—I can never talk to her."

"Yes, you can; she won't want much talk-

ing, and you had better send her to bed soon.
You must make the effort, Gertrude; for Sir
Henry's sake and your own."

Thus encouraged, Gertrude went trembling
to Lady Amy's room, and Leonie proceeded
to the drawing-room. She first announced aloud
that Lady Kincardine had taken her place by
Lady Amy, and then privately informed Sir
Henry of the real state of the case.   He, for
his part, was so calm, so like his usual self,
that none could have believed he had any cause
for anxiety, or had to solve the pleasing pro-
blem of how he was immediately to raise
£4000 without borrowing.   His self-com-
mand was wonderful.   Never had he been
more lively, or more devoted to his guests'
amusement; every person seemed to feel
himself the object of his special attention;
and the general remark at the end of the evening was, how very agreeable Sir Henry
had been, and what good spirits he had
been in.

The next morning came the inspection of
the accounts, and a sad business it proved to
be.   Such a tale of extravagance and folly

never had been seen; and Sir Henry's brow darkened as he looked over long dress-makers' bills, milliners', florists', shoemakers', &c., and memorandums of exorbitant sums spent on costly and unnecessary nick-nacks. Worst of all was the bill for the fancy Court-dress. He perfectly remembered being told that it was to cost a hundred pounds, and having remonstrated against that as extravagant; and behold, when he came to add up the different items, including the fan, and resetting of the jewels, it came to more than four hundred! He said nothing, but merely pointed to the list of figures.

"Yes—I know—and I know what I promised you," said Gertrude, mournfully. "Indeed, Henry, I meant to keep my word; I had no idea how much I was spending."

"There it is," said Sir Henry, "you never have any idea how much you are spending. This can't go on. Do you know how much you have spent on your dress for the last six years,—ever since I took office, and we went to London regularly, that is?"

"Indeed I can't tell."

"Fifteen hundred a year, more or less; and this year, including this last sum, it comes to four thousand. Before that, it was seven hundred a year. And your pin-money—all I am bound to give you by your marriage settlements—is four hundred."

Gertrude crimsoned with shame.

"Oh, Henry! how can I ever look you in the face again?" she said, hanging down her head, and hiding her face in her hands.

"Well—you never find much difficulty in that," said Sir Henry, with a slight smile. "But I tell you what it is; there must be an end of this;—we must come to an understanding. Now listen. For the future I will give you a thousand a year, on the distinct understanding that you pay all your own bills; I will have no extras."

"That is too much," said Gertrude; "I will only have the four hundred to which I am entitled."

"With your expensive tastes, it would be perfect nonsense to attempt managing on four hundred; a mere temptation to run into fresh debts and difficulties. Besides, I can afford a thousand a year, and while I can, I don't want you to deny yourself anything reasonable and fair."

"Oh, Henry! your kindness heaps coals of fire on my head! But I can't let you redeem these diamonds. If you will advance the money, I will pay it by instalments. You shall only give me five hundred a year till it is paid."

Sir Henry considered, and presently came to the conclusion that it would be no bad thing for Gertrude to pay some part of the money herself, and be an evident relief to the overwhelming sense of shame by which she was oppressed.

"You will never be able to pay it all," he said. "But if you like to pay me some part of it by instalments, you can do so; but I shall give you the full thousand, and you must take out for yourself what you can afford. Only don't consider yourself in any way bound, and if you find you can't save anything, don't worry yourself about it. But now I come to the last item, and what it is I don't clearly

understand. 'Paid Miss Wood £75.' Who
is Miss Wood?"

"Oh, that is the worst of all! that is a terrible business! Miss Wood was Geraldine Lawrance's governess. You know I lived with
Uncle and Aunt Bournemouth for three years
while papa and mamma were in the West
Indies; and all that time Miss Wood was very
kind to me, and took great pains with me.
Well, poor thing, four years ago she lost her
health, had to leave the situation which she
then had, and was entirely destitute. Geraldine, if she had known about it, could not have
helped her; I heard of her distress, and
promised to give her fifty pounds a year till
she was able to go out again."

" Which was taking a burden upon yourself that did not belong to you," observed
Sir Henry, parenthetically. "Bournemouth
was the proper person to assist her, and
would, no doubt, have been glad to do it,
if you had applied to him."

" I can't say I paid it regularly," said
Gertrude, colouring as she proceeded; "still
it was always paid every year at one time

or another, till two years ago, when I was only able to pay half; and after that for eighteen months I never paid anything at all, till I accidentally heard that she was in the most dreadful distress for this very money; and it was the horror I felt at finding what she had suffered that made me go off at once and pawn the diamonds."

" Indeed, Gertrude, this is very bad," said Sir Henry; " for her sake you should have applied to me. Though, as I said before, Bournemouth is the proper person to help her, I would pay anything rather than that a promise of that sort should be broken, especially to a person who had been kind to you. Is there anything owing her for this year ? "

" No—I paid this about five months ago."

" That is all, then? Have you any debts or bills of any description ? "

" Not one."

" Then if I pay you two hundred and fifty pounds on New Year's day, you will start clear."

" Quite clear."

" Very well; then remember our agreement, and let me have no more bills. I must consider now about redeeming these diamonds, for what with my moors having let badly, and being irregularly paid, and the new road to Pitmuir, and one thing and another, I have really no ready money left, beyond what is necessary for the household expenses."

" Oh, Henry, I am so sorry! indeed I am!" said Gertrude.

" My dear Gertrude, say no more about it. What's done can't be undone, and we must make the best of it. I am sure you are sorry now; but whether you will really succeed in restraining your extravagant tastes, is a question I may well feel doubtful about. But if you do get into debt again, you positively must get yourself out."

And Sir Henry gathered up all the bills and walked away, with the air of a man who has a great burden on his shoulders, but means to bear it like a man, stoutly and in silence.

Gertrude now felt it incumbent on her

to ascertain what her guests were doing, and to pay a visit to Lady Amy, who was very much better, but had not come down to breakfast, by Lady Bournemouth's advice. Later in the day she communicated to Leonie the result of her interview with Sir Henry, not omitting anything.

· " Oh, my dear Gertrude, how could you?" exclaimed Leonie, as she came to the part about Miss Wood. "If you had told us, we should have been only too happy to pay it. Where is this lady? Is fifty pounds a year enough for her?"

" Yes, I think so; and I believe she is better; the last time she wrote to me she said something about hoping to be able to resume teaching. So I promised to let her know if I heard of anything likely to suit her. I wish you would help me, for you are just as likely to be in the way of such things as I am."

"I will keep it in mind, and write to you if I succeed in finding any situation that sounds promising. How is Amy?"

" Very much better; I am thankful to

say there is nothing to prevent her leaving
with the Burleighs, the day after to-morrow,
though her arm is still in a sling. Oh, dear
me! how glad I shall be when all these
people are gone, and there are only you
two and Willie left! We shall have the
house to ourselves the day after to-morrow.
It will be very dull for you, I am afraid,
but really I cannot entertain people when
my head is full of this miserable business!"

"I can quite understand that; and you
need not be afraid for us. Lindon is at
present devoted to curling, and I see no
prospect of the frost breaking. And I dare
say you and I shall amuse ourselves tolerably
together. At all events, if you make yourself unpleasant, we can go home."

"I will try to stop short of forcing that
remedy upon you," said Gertrude.

"Leonie," said Lord Bournemouth to his
wife, when he came to her room before
dressing, "Gertrude and Henry have had
a row!"

"Why do you think so?"

" Oh, I see it plainly enough; though, to do them justice, they keep up appearances tolerably. What was it about? Come, out with it."

" Well, to tell the truth, Sir Henry found out that she has been exceedingly extravagant, and has pawned her diamonds to pay her bills."

" Whew—ew—," whistled Lord Bournemouth; " and they are not hers either, for you told me yourself they were family diamonds. Pretty cool that, I must say! Didn't I tell you there would be a row? What did Henry say?"

" Sir Henry behaved exceedingly well, with a kindness and forbearance that even I did not expect from him. She has shown him all her accounts, and they have settled it between them."

" And the diamonds?"

" He is going to redeem them himself."

" How much is it?"

" Four thousand pounds."

" Whew — ew —," again whistled Lord

Bournemouth, " do you mean to say that Gertrude has spent four thousand pounds on her finery in one year ? "

" Four ;—four hundred for her allowance, six hundred for some bills that Sir Henry paid in the spring and summer."

" I'm glad I didn't marry her ! " was Lord Bournemouth's next observation.

" Did you ever think of doing so ? " inquired Leonie, quickly.

Lord Bournemouth saw that he had betrayed himself, coloured slightly, laughed, and said, " I don't know why I should be ashamed to own it; I did once."

" Did you propose ? " said Leonie.

" No—it never went as far as that ; I was thinking of it, when my mother put me up to the state of my father's affairs, and, as Gertrude hadn't a penny,—figuratively speaking, for her fortune was only five thousand,—I saw it wouldn't do, packed up my things, took leave of my disconsolate family, set off for America— and you know what happened there. Seriously though, Leonie," said Lord Bournemouth, dropping his careless tone, " I hope you don't think from this that I married you for your money?"

"If I was not convinced of that by this time," said Leonie with a smile, "I think our marriage would have been rather a failure. But now you are in the humour for confidences, tell me one thing more."

"Well?"

"Why did you wait so long before proposing?" said Leonie, looking shyly up, with a smile on her lips, and a beautiful pink flush on her face.

"Oh, you wretch!" exclaimed Lord Bourne-mouth, laughing immoderately; "then you were expecting my proposal?"

"Of course I was;—remember, I had been married before."

"True; that is an advantage I never enjoyed, and therefore was not up to the ways of the thing."

"On your honour now, why was it?"

"On my honour, Leonie, it was your money that stood in my way. I left my father's house, meaning, if ever I married at all, to marry a woman with a large fortune, but somehow when I came face to face with you, and the thing was to be done, it had an ugly look, and I didn't like it."

" How did you get over the plainness of its aspect? " inquired Leonie, quaintly.

" Because there was no plainness in yours, I suppose. Not that I married you for your face either, though it is a tidy one; or for your wits, or your accomplishments."

" For what then? For the charms of my character and disposition? " said Leonie, drawing down the corners of her mouth.

" Not that either! though I'd challenge Europe to show a woman that would beat you. But because you were Leonie de Sosada, and no one else, I suppose."

" I am satisfied," said Leonie, " that is how I wish to be loved."

" Well, but what is Henry to do in future? He can't go on paying up at this rate? "

" No, he is to give her a thousand a year, and compounds for no bills."

" And a nice sum, too, for a woman to spend on her clothes alone, for I'll be bound she does nothing else with it. Why, I don't suppose you spend a couple of hundreds on yours."

" A couple of hundreds ! no. If I am extravagant, about a hundred and fifty or sixty ; but generally one hundred, or rather over."

" And you look every bit as well dressed as she does. But you are one in a thousand for managing."

" Ah, by the bye, talking about managing, have you heard from your agent again ? "

" From Newby ? I had a long letter from him this morning, and things seem going on pretty well in our parts. Caldwell Farm sold well, so we shall have that money in hand."

" That was the outlying farm, that we settled was more trouble than it was worth. What do you mean to do with the money ? "

" That is just the question. There is so much to be done, that it is difficult to say what should come first. I must have a new cottage or two, I think."

" Yes, do ; for the village is sadly crowded. We can talk it over, and settle the sites and plans when we return."

" And we must see about the School-house,
and there are those farm houses to be looked
into. I must consider, too, about making that
bridge near Cranston, which seems greatly
needed. What a bore it all is! Nature never
could have meant me for a landed proprietor."

" And why not? We don't always find
ourselves where we like best to be. I did not
like being a slave-holder."

" And you did not remain one."

" I will not discuss the question, for I
have no time at present; and it always re-
mains that you are a landed proprietor, and
can't become anything else. Here is a letter
from Arthur, which Geraldine enclosed to me
to-day; I have only just finished it."

" Let us see what he says," said Lord
Bournemouth, settling himself comfortably in
an arm-chair. " I so seldom have a line
from him that, if it were not for Geraldine's letters, we should never have an idea
what he is about. My sweetest of Cherry-
blossoms,—to be sure, how fond the boy is

of her! This seems very satisfactory; there
is nothing about disliking his profession
now, and apparently he is making some
friends."

"Yes," said Leonie, "there has been a
gradual improvement in the whole tone of
his letters. They seem to want Lord Ernest
out there; I wish he would go back, for
they evidently don't like Major Conyngham,
and I am afraid of Arthur's taking a dis-
gust to the army."

"You are perfectly barbarous," returned
Lord Bournemouth; "the poor fellow has
only just recovered from that wound, and
barely got up his strength again. I am
sure he is not one to shirk. Arthur was
fortunate in getting into his regiment, and
fortunate in being ordered abroad, and not
left with the depôt. I was not sorry he was
disgusted at first, for it wouldn't have been a
particularly good sign if he had been satisfied
with the life and society of ordinary country
quarters."

"Very true," said Leonie. "I am sure

he will turn out thoroughly well. I like his letters of all things ; they are so acute, and, at the same time, so fresh and original. The description of his manner of living and pursuits is exceedingly amusing."

"And what capital sketches these are he has made in the corner of his paper ! I hope he will cultivate this turn for drawing; I dare say it will be useful some day. Yes —this is a hopeful letter enough ; I think the boy means to be a credit to the family. Perhaps we shall all live to plume ourselves on being related to General Sir Arthur Vivian; who knows ? I wish he would write to me oftener, for though I see all Geraldine's letters, I think I should know more about him and his ways if he wrote to me direct-ly. That is never the dressing-bell ring-ing ? "

"Indeed it is ; so pray go at once, for I want to dress."

"I say—what a way Geraldine will be in when she hears of this business of Ger-trude's ! " said Lord Bournemouth, stopping short at the door.

" Pray don't write about it to her, but wait till we return."

" All right. She would only worry herself about it sooner then necessary."

The next day the frost had so far broken that curling or skating was out of the question; therefore Sir Henry proposed to his guests that they should take their guns, and see what game could be shot.

" I can't promise you much sport," he said, " but we may pick up a few woodcocks ; and, at all events, there are the blue hares."

Captain Kincardine, being missed at the breakfast table, was found to have started at break of day, accompanied by an under-keeper, in pursuit of some wild geese, which had been seen the day before about eight miles off ; stragglers, apparently, from a large flock on its way southwards. Sir Henry secretly envied him and pitied himself; as he hated shooting with a large party, and the " wild goose chase " presented difficulties and fatigues, and required perseverance and energy enough to please even him.

Gertrude was left with the task of amusing the

ladies on her hands, and was very much at a
loss how to do it. Usually she was equal to
any social emergency of the description, but
on this occasion she did not feel equal to the
exertion, and was besides vexed and disappointed at the departure of Sir James Pen-
nant, who had been unexpectedly summoned
to London. She sat in the drawing-room,
fidgeting with a piece of work, and trying to
talk, in which she succeeded palpably ill, more
especially as she was considering all the time
what she should do with Mr Kinghorn, who
was hanging about the ladies, looking disconsolate. At last she bethought herself of asking
him to read some poetry aloud, then improved
upon that by putting a volume of his own
poems into his hand, saying that they were
charming and delicious, but she was sure she
should appreciate them a thousand times more
if she heard them read aloud, especially by
their author—of course no one could read
them as well as the person who had composed
them; at which the young man looked might-
ily pleased, and Leonie shook her head, and
whispered, " If Sir James could see you now,

he would never introduce you to his friend."

Whereupon Gertrude put on a comical look of penitence, and replied, "But what can I do? He is so silly, and really I can flatter him so nicely."

Then Margaret Chetwynd fell into raptures at the poems, and entered into a long metaphysical discussion with Mr Kinghorn, in which they both went hopelessly out of their depth, and plunged about in a ring, becoming more involved and confused, and talking greater twaddle and nonsense every minute, till Lady Arabella Burleigh and Mrs Tredegar went to sleep, and Gertrude's head ached. Leonie had turned her thoughts off to Avonbury, and was engaged in a mental calculation of how much money it would take to build an almshouse, to contain twelve men and twelve women. Georgie Kincardine and Lady Amy had stolen away, and were playing at battledore and shuttlecock in the great hall together, Lady Amy running about and enjoying the game like a very child, and demonstrating by voice and example that she could play with her left hand just as well as with her right.

"I would not be Gertrude," observed Georgie, "Margaret would just drive me daft."

"Nor I neither; we are much better off. Here comes Captain Kincardine. I wonder what sport he has had."

Captain Kincardine looked very grave, and was very silent when he came in, notwithstanding his assurances that he had had excellent sport, far better than he had hoped for. Georgie thought he was tired, and so he was, but nevertheless he did not seem able to rest, but wandered about, round the house, and up the path, down which the other gentlemen might be expected to return. He went to meet them as soon as they were in sight, and, joining Sir Henry, contrived to separate him from the others.

"Harry, what's all this?" he said. "Fraser says you are not going to buy Glenachrie after all!"

"Fraser is quite right, I have given it up."

"But, Harry, you have wanted it ever since I can remember! It just makes the property perfect on that side. You will never have such a chance again."

" I know that, Willie ; but I can't afford it."

" I thought you had the money ready ! "

" So I had ; but I have now another use for it."

Captain Kincardine was confounded. Ever since he could remember, it had been his father's wish, and after that his brother's, to buy this property, which had never been in the market before. Though of little value in itself, it became so from the fact of its standing in the middle of the Kincardine estate, and every offer had been made to induce the proprietor to part with it. He, a sturdy old Highlander, would not hear of alienating the land which had descended to him from many generations of ancestors ; but on his death his son, an extravagant, reckless young man, offered it to Sir Henry. And now Sir Henry, after waiting for it for twenty years, was not going to buy it ! It was inconceivable !

" Are you in difficulties ? " he said at last. " I wish you would tell me what it is all about, for I dare say I could help you if you are in a scrape."

"Thank you, Willie; but it's of no use. I am in a scrape, and you can't help me out of it. What sport did you have?"

"Very good—I shot three geese, and Will Roy too. How did you shoot?"

"Pretty well;—Ernest Fitzgermaine shot best on the whole, though Tredegar wasn't bad either. But we might have had another gun; I was rather sorry you were not with us, though I dare say you had better fun."

"I hope you didn't want Will Roy?" said Captain Kincardine, quickly.

"Oh no, you know I told you he is always at your disposal. What a muff Chetwynd is!"

"He must have been a muff to marry Margaret," replied Captain Kincardine, argumentatively; "no man in his senses would tie himself with such a blue stocking."

"Lady Bournemouth is just as learned as Margaret, and Bournemouth is not by any means a muff."

"It's not learning makes a woman blue, any

more than it is bad shooting makes a man a muff—always. How those hares are blown to pieces! That's Chetwynd's handiwork, I'll lay anything."

" True for you, Willie, that one is Chetwynd's, but that is Mowbray's, who was in such a hurry to cut him out, that he fired at any distance or no distance. Such wild work you never saw. I thought some of our heads would have been blown off between them."

" I shan't ask him again. One must bear with one's brother-in-law, I suppose, but there's no need to bear with him."

" Well," said Captain Kincardine, " if Georgie ever thinks of marrying such a noodle as Chetwynd, or such a puppy as Mowbray, I shall do the heavy father, and forbid the banns."

" It would be a great pity to see Georgie so thrown away," said Sir Henry, thoughtfully. "Margaret deteriorates every year. Why I was weak enough to give my consent, I can't conceive, for, with her looks and money, she might have done far better."

" Bless you, Harry, you could no more have

prevented Margaret's marrying Chetwynd, than you could prevent Chetwynd's blowing this wretched woodcock into a hundred bits. A nice house we should have had of it till you gave your consent."

" There 's something in that," said Sir Henry. " I see Gertrude looking out of the library window. Will you go and tell her that the two Grants and McDonald are coming to dinner, whilst I put by my gun ? "

Captain Kincardine glanced up at the window, then, as if seized with a sudden idea, shot off without saying a word, rushed up to the library, and strolled leisurely in, with his hands in his pockets.

" Well ! what an explosive boy that is ! " soliloquized Sir Henry, as he walked off in the direction of the gun-room, " what is he up to now ? "

Captain Kincardine looked carefully round the room, and seeing no one but Gertrude there, delivered his message, then took up the papers which had just come in.

" What news ? " said Gertrude. " Can you

see to read them? You had better ring for the lamps."

"Not for me, thank you. I'm going to smoke a cigar in a second. What news? None that I can see. Funds dropped again; I'm glad I sold out when I did. What's this? To be sold—farm of 500 acres—well stocked; sounds well for those who like the kind of thing. By the bye," he continued carelessly, "why has Harry given up buying Glenachrie?"

"Given up buying Glenachrie! where is that?"

"The land in the middle of the property which my father always meant to buy. Now it is offered to Harry, he won't have it, though he had the money ready a short time ago. Do you know why?"

"Oh, indeed I do," said Gertrude, in a tone of the greatest distress; "a great deal too well. Oh, my dear Willie, can't it be arranged? It's all my fault!"

"Your fault? how so?" inquired Willie, putting down the paper.

"It's all my wicked extravagance? I have brought him into difficulties—I have pawned the diamonds—and now he must give this money to redeem them! Oh, what shall I do?"

"Do? nothing. It appears to me that you've done a great deal too much already," said Willie, with the slightest possible shade of contempt in his voice, and on his handsome face.

"I know you despise me," said Gertrude mournfully, and hardly able to restrain her tears, "every one must; but do advise me; do tell me if nothing can be done."

Captain Kincardine did despise her; the woman did not exist whom he would have thought good enough for his brother, and Gertrude fell particularly short of his standard, more especially since this last sin, a capital one in his eyes. Still, her voice of distress might have mollified a stone, and he replied, "Don't cry; Harry will be in presently, and he hates red eyes, and all that sort of thing. What did you receive for them?"

"Three thousand."

"What a bad bargain you drove, to be sure!" returned Willie, stroking his moustache reflectively. "However, it's all the better for us. Perhaps diamonds are down in the market; they're ticklish things, up one day and down the next. There, don't cry, Gertrude; I didn't mean to vex you, and, after all, it's just as well that you only got three thousand. I think I see my way out of this business. I'll step down to the gun-room, find Harry, and see if I can't settle it."

"Oh, thank you, dear Willie! I can never be grateful enough."

"Well, after all, it's for Harry, you know," said Captain Kincardine, unwilling to let her suppose that he did it for herself.

He went down to the gun-room, and found Sir Henry handling and admiring the wild geese.

"Come away, Harry, I want a word with you," he said. "So Gertrude tells me she has brought you into this scrape."

"You have not been asking her?" exclaim-ed Sir Henry.

"Yes, I have; at least I asked her why

you were going to give up buying the farm, and she truly observed that she knew a great deal too well.　So don't blow up, Harry, for it's too late."

This was said with such perfect coolness and unconcern, that Sir Henry, who was prepared to be seriously angry, burst out laughing.

" Ah—it's not quite a subject for laughter, either," said Captain Kincardine.　"Now I tell you what, Harry; to make a short story of it, I have more than three thousand pounds on my hands just now, and you are welcome to as much of it as you want, for as long as you want; only pray buy Glenachrie, for you won't have another chance."

" Willie!" said Sir Henry, "thank you with all my heart, my good fellow; it's extremely kind of you, but I couldn't think of accepting it."

" And why not, pray? Just listen to me. I sold out two months ago, in order to buy my Captaincy, when meanwhile poor Fendie died, and I got the step without purchase.　Since then, the funds have been so high that I have never bought in again, so there it is doing nothing; and why should not you have it?"

"The funds are down again; why don't you buy in, or invest in something else? There are a good many advantageous investments to be made just now."

"The funds are still too high; I should buy in at too great a loss; and not likely to drop enough for me yet, I'm told. And I have ten thousand invested in Railway Debentures, and bringing me in $8\frac{1}{2}$ per cent.; so I prefer to have five thousand in the funds, that there may be something to fall back upon, should the other smash, not but what it's perfectly secure, I believe. So come, Harry; let us have no more fuss about it."

"It's perfectly secure with me," said Sir Henry, musingly; "for though the estate is strictly entailed, it can be secured to you on the personality, should I die suddenly. If all goes well, I can pay it you in the course of this next year; it is only for the present that I'm pressed; and I am determined that these wretched diamonds shall not stay in pawn a day longer than I can help. I will give you five per cent. interest."

"Interest!" said Captain Kincardine, "do you take me for a money-lender that I should ask interest from you? Who paid my debts, and made me a present of my commission, that I might have my fortune clear? Don't talk to me about interest."

"This will never do, Willie," said Sir Henry, decidedly; "if you don't let me pay you interest, I won't borrow it. We are both men of business, and know the world, and know that the obligation is great enough already, if I do pay you five per cent. for it."

"The obligation would be all on my side," said Captain Kincardine, "for I have already shown you that I can't get five per cent. for it."

"What will you let me pay you then? The same that you would get in the funds? If you don't agree at least to this, I can have nothing more to do with it."

"I must, if you won't take it on any other terms; though why such a trifling sum is to

be such a mighty matter between us, I confess
I can't see. Well, then, I may consider that
settled? You will buy the land?"

" Only too glad, and thank you very much,
Willie; you have conferred a very great obligation on me."

And Sir Henry shook his brother's hand
warmly, with a sort of embarrassment very
different from, and far more agreeable than, his
usual stately composure.

" Oh well, there's no great obligation, so the
less said about it the better," was the answer.

" It will take a load off poor Gertrude's
mind," said Sir Henry; "I must go and tell
her at once."

At which Captain Kincardine walked off in
an opposite direction, slightly cross, and
muttering to himself, " Gertrude! Always
Gertrude! Well, it's all right, I suppose, and
no business of mine either; but I wish it was
always Harry, and then we shouldn't have had
such a piece of work."

Gertrude's delight and relief were fully
shown in her gaiety and bright sparkling
manner that evening. The dancing seemed

to be kept up with greater spirit, the music to
be more lively, and everybody to enjoy themselves more.   Leonie played with untiring zeal
for more than an hour, and then Georgie Kincardine took her place.   Lady Amy St Aubyn
could neither dance nor play; her arm was
still in a sling, but she did not appear to consider it a privation; for Captain Kincardine
sat beside her almost the whole evening, and,
to judge by her frequent hearty laughs, his
conversation was very agreeable.   Lord
Bournemouth announced himself to be far
too old to dance ; then, with his usual good-
nature, finding that gentlemen were really
wanted, looked round, and selected the ugliest
girl in the room as his partner, who was there-
by made happy for the rest of the evening.
He was afterwards claimed by Gertrude, who
had been watching the dancers with longing eyes,
but did not chose to waltz with any one but
Sir Henry, Captain Kincardine, or her cousin.
Lady Arabella Burleigh seemed perfectly satisfied with Mr Tredegar's attentions ; more
especially as, before the evening was over, he
had asked her and Mr Burleigh to his place in

Wales, and she had cajoled him into promising her a mount on his best hunter, to the pre- judice of Mrs Tredegar, who accordingly registered a little vow of vengeance. Little Lady Amy, after a time, most unselfishly left her pleasant companion, and devoted herself to a poor deaf and dumb boy, who had established a kind of claim on her, as being a third or fourth cousin, and was supposed to find some amusement in going out to parties, though what it would be difficult to say. She showed him prints, contrived by ingenuity and diligence, and a system of clever little signs, to make him understand her, and to understand him in return ; interpreted his wish for a cup of tea to the servants, and altogether made him perfectly happy, and amused him more than, poor fellow, he had been for many a long day.

Then, as Captain Kincardine observed, " Henry patronized reels," by which he did not mean that his brother performed therein, but that he found partners for all who wanted them, and looked on, much in the fashion of a high-caste Spaniard assisting at the dances of

a set of Indians or Aztecs. Margaret Chetwynd had established herself in a corner of
the room with Messrs Elston and Kinghorn,
and discussed Shakspeare — the musical
glasses being out of fashion now-a-days—and,
for once in a way, Gertrude was sincerely
thankful to her for taking them off her hands.
And so the evening passed off, and left some
results behind it ; of which we will give one
specimen.

"Harry, I want your advice," were the
words which Sir Henry heard, as he stood before his dressing-room fire, with his back to
the door; and turning round, found that his
brother had come in without knocking.

" What about ?" he said, pulling off his
coat, and throwing it into a chair.

" What should you think of my marrying ?"

This required consideration, so Sir Henry
pulled off his right boot, and kicked it across
the room before he answered, " You are full
young to marry, and you know I think a man
in the army is far better unmarried; but of
course it would depend very much on the
person."

" What should you say to Amy St Aubyn ?"

The left boot followed the right one, the feet had been thrust into a pair of slippers, and a dressing-gown assumed, before Sir Henry replied, " You might do worse."

Captain Kincardine, who knew his brother, was neither provoked at the delay, nor at the moderation of the answer when it did come, but continued, " I haven't proposed yet ; but I am pretty certain she will have me."

" So am I, for that matter," returned Sir Henry, smiling. " But before we go any further, let me ask if you have thought about money ?"

" I'm not an absolute idiot," was the somewhat irrelevant proposition which followed. " She has five thousand, and I have fifteen thousand and my commission, so I think we should be able to manage. She is not an extravagant girl in her tastes, I think ; for I've watched her pretty closely, one time and another. What should you say ?"

The question was put with such earnestness and anxiety, that Sir Henry hastened to answer, as he could with perfect sincerity, " I

should not think she was—and, to tell you the
truth, I think she would rather rough it a little
with you than live at home without you."

"At home ! h'm—it's not a very pleasant
place for her, or any of them, I suspect, and
that, you see, makes a difference."

"It does," said Sir Henry, "and, really, she
is a particularly nice girl ; very good-tempered,
and very unselfish and amiable."

"That's just it," said Willie, eagerly, "and
when I saw her to-night, taking care of that
poor fellow, young what d' you call him?—talking to him—how she managed it, goodness
only knows, as if he were the best fun in the
world, it struck me more than ever that that's
the sort of girl I should like for my wife."

"It is a good sign that you think more of
her character than her face," said Sir Henry,
"though that's by no means amiss."

"Amiss ! I should think not ! " said Captain
Kincardine indignantly, "and then her riding
is undeniable—such a hand as she has on a
horse, and her figure is perfection in a habit ;
and, upon my word, I do think that little face
of hers under her riding hat, with the bit of

black feather hanging down by it, the prettiest thing in the world."

" Now look here, Willie," said Sir Henry, " I'm quite willing to listen to all your raptures; in fact, it would be positive cruelty to stop you, but let us do it methodically."

He sat down, drew his chair close to the fire, took a cigar case off the chimney-piece, opened it, took out the single cigar which remained, and observed, " Only one left. You see that cigar?"

" Well—yes—it's a pretty big one, if you come to that."

" It is; I should be sorry to stint you. Till that cigar is smoked out, you may talk as much as you please; after that, I'm going to bed."

The manner, quite as much as the matter of this speech, might have disconcerted some men, but Willie Kincardine was on too intimate terms with his brother to be disconcerted by anything he said; so he merely observed :

". What have you done with the others?"

" They are down-stairs in the smoking room, at least I hope so; and really, old fellow, it's

so long since you and I have had a regular
good gossip together, that I shall just leave
them there, and not* trouble my head about
them. I'm sorry I have not another cigar at
hand for you, but perhaps you have one about
you ; or, at any rate, you will prefer talking."

"I think I shall propose to-morrow," observed Willie. "I'd rather have it settled at
once. Suppose she refuses me ? "

"More fool she. We'll keep our own counsel, Willie."

Sir Henry's sentences, never very long, became curter and more sententious when they
had to be jerked out, with a cigar between his
teeth. "Let me give you one piece of advic e.
Give her an allowance, and don't have any
bills."

"Bills! don't talk of them!" said Willie ;
" I've had enough of my own, though, thanks.
to you, Harry, I am quite straight now. What
a bore it would be if I were in difficulties just
when I want to marry! Well, Amy won't
have any diamonds to pawn, thank goodness,
unless her own people give her some, for I

shan't. And she looks all the better for being plainly dressed; all thorough-breds do. It's all in the cut and the colour, good dressing is, only it is astonishing how few people know it. I could make my fortune if I set up as a tailor. There is not one in London who can cut a pair of trousers, except Rigby; I might have a monopoly in that article alone."

"You puppy!" growled Sir Henry. "Is Lady Amy to set up as a mantua maker, or whatever they call it, at the same time?"

"If she does, I shall get Gertrude to buy her things there, and you to pay the bills," was the cool answer. "But Amy would never be able to put on all the ribbons and snippery that Gertrude wears; she would addle her poor little brains in the attempt. Rather a contrast our two wives will be; one for use, and one for show."

"H'm—I conclude the useful one is yours; pray to what particular use do you mean to put her?"

"I knew a man who made his wife groom his horse," returned Willie. "I dare say Amy could turn her hand to that, if we were put to it ; only if they blew their noses, she would be blown away.   But it is surprising what pluck the mite has ;—little and good, as they say."

" I never saw any one behave more pluckily than she did when she fell down on the ice," said Sir Henry, willing to please his brother. " You could not have guessed she was hurt at all."

" Poor child ! what a tumble it must have been ; I never saw such a sight as her shoulder is even now.   By the bye, I wonder if Ernest Fitzgermaine has any idea of marrying."

" At what a tangent you do go off ! " said Sir Henry, taking the end of his cigar out of his mouth, and throwing it into the fire. " Because you are going to be married, do you suppose every one else is ? "

" No—but he has money enough now to do so, and they say he wished it at one time."

" What made you think of him now ? With his present prospects I dare say he would have no difficulty, if there is any young lady in view.   But I have heard of none."

" Nor I,—the fact is, it was a passing fraternal thought for Georgie."

" You needn't think of that," said Sir Henry, " there is not the slightest chance of anything of the sort on either side ; though I should be only too glad if there was."

" Ever since Margaret made such a hash of her affairs, I have been in terror lest Georgie should do the same."

" What it is to stand *in loco parentis* to a couple of girls ! " said Captain Kincardine. " I am glad I did not come into a ready-made young family at twenty-one."

" You appear to think the girls the worst part of the business," retorted Sir Henry ; "now I seem to remember various troubles and worries caused by a certain young gentleman who utterly refused to become acquainted with the limits of his allowance."

" And uncommonly well you behaved when I was undergoing the process of cultivating wild oats," said Captain Kincardine, reddening. " I wonder what I should have turned out, but for you."

" Not but for me," said Sir Henry, gravely ;

"nothing but God's mercy set you straight then, and has kept you straight ever since. You were going downwards pretty fast, in spite of me."

" That's true, but honour to whom honour is due, and you come next, as my earthly providence ; dear old boy that you are ! "

· Sir Henry answered this burst of enthusiasm with a grave smile, and glance of quiet affection, and then said, " Well, my cigar has been out some time ; I have been better than my word. You will let me know how it goes with Lady Amy ; I shall be glad to hear that it is all right."

Will our readers be glad to hear it too ? If so, they shall have that satisfaction, for it was all right ; not only with Lady Amy, but with all her family. The wedding took place in six weeks, and neither Captain Kincardine nor Amy ever had reason to repent of their choice. They were abundantly happy and abundantly prosperous.

After this evening, the party at Kincardine gradually broke up ; Captain Kincardine went to London to arrange his money affairs with a

view to accommodating his brother, and facili-
tating his own marriage; Leonie and Lord
Bournemouth returned to Avonbury. The
rest of the guests dispersed, some to their own
homes, others to different country houses.
Lord Ernest sailed at once for the Cape,
where his presence was beginning to be much
needed, and from time to time reports reached
England through the despatches, and various
private sources, of his rapid and steady rise
there. His unconquerable energy and sound
judgment had already made themselves felt
and valued, and now his talent and fertility of
resource were everywhere acknowledged and
appreciated. The command of a district,
which he obtained at this time, by enlarging
his sphere, brought these qualities into public
notice, to the delight of such of his friends
as had always known that they existed, and
only required an opportunity for developing
themselves. Those around him could alone
fully appreciate his skill, calculation, and un-
wavering perseverance, but all could understand his more daring and brilliant actions.
Ernest Fitzgermaine's name became a sy-

nonym for courage and heroism, for deeds
which might equal those of the knights of old,
and soon all England rang with his praise.
Men began to talk to one another of the great
things that might be expected from him,
should a war of more serious importance
break out, to discuss the honours that would
probably be conferred upon him, and to predict that he would be the founder of another
warrior family, and leave a hard-earned coro-
net to his children. We shall see. We have
looked forward a few years because it is more
convenient to do so now, our story lying for
the present somewhat apart from him and his
services and exploits. But we must not
wander too far. We have said enough to
connect and explain any incidental mention
that may be made of him for the present, and
the end will be shown in due time.

CHAPTER II.

I tell you rather, that, whoever may
Discern true ends here, shall grow pure enough
To love them, brave enough to strive for them,
And strong enough to reach them, though the roads
    be rough.   E. BARRETT BROWNING.

She was weak and frail,
She could not bear the joy of giving life—
The mother-rapture slew her. If her kiss
Had left a longer weight upon my lips,
It might have steadied the uneasy breath,
And reconciled and fraternized my soul
With the new order. As it was, indeed,
I felt a mother-want about the world,
And still went seeking, like a bleating lamb
Left out at night in shutting up the fold—
As restless as a nest-deserted bird,
Grown chill through something being awry, tho' what
It knows not.   E. BARRETT BROWNING.

AVONBURY looks cheerful and inhabited
now, for three and a half years have passed

since we were with Gertrude at Kincardine
Castle, and Lord and Lady Bournemouth have
gone into their house. A very pleasant, comfortable house it is, well, but not too well fur-
nished, for luxury is what neither Leonie nor
her husband would wish; more, it must be
owned, from duty than from inclination. Lord
Bournemouth has begun in earnest among his
tenantry, and a good work is doing there. He
is indefatigable in his exertions, originating all
sorts of schemes for himself, helping Leonie in
all hers, and sparing neither time, money, nor
trouble. No one in the world, except his wife,
could tell what this cost him. His natural in-
dolence was such that the slightest exertion
was a worry and annoyance to him, and it
was only the strongest and most conscientious
sense of duty that determined him to give
himself entirely to the work. If he had had
his own will, the sort of life he would have enjoyed would have been roaming over the world
with Leonie, unencumbered by any cares or
duties, staying where and when, and for how
long, it pleased him, moving from any place
directly he was tired of it, returning to Eng-

land now and then for sporting, unbound by
any ties to any one country. His present
mode of life was utterly hateful to him;
cottages and their occupants an abomination
in his eyes, and schools a weariness to the
flesh. It was all, as he said himself, "one
long pull against collar." But so earnestly
did he endeavour to do his duty, so resolutely
and cheerfully did he " put on the harness,"
that no one but Leonie guessed the real state
of the case. It was a common remark in the
neighbourhood and among his friends, that,
" though it was true Lord Bournemouth gave
up most of his time to his people, yet it was
really no sacrifice to him, he so completely
found his enjoyment in it. And, after all, one
always did see that people employed themselves in the manner that suited them best,
and quite right too."

Leonie, for her part, was far more in her
element than her husband. We have before
heard her inveigh pretty strongly against an
English country-house life; but he, remember-
ing her opinions, took care that she should
never know the dulness and stagnation she so

much dreaded. He rightly thought that with
her peculiar education, with her intellect, and
thirst for intellectual society, it would have
been positive cruelty to shut her up in the
country, without a creature with whom to speak,
except the neighbours, who were not only few,
but insipid. So Avonbury was constantly
filled with a succession of guests, and guests of
the best class. All the leading men of the day
—and women too—all those of the fashion-
able world remarkable for something else besides fashion and frivolity, were to be found
there. All arts and sciences, all shades and
sections of opinion and thought, had their re-
presentatives at Avonbury Castle, and were
all duly appreciated by their hostess and her
husband.

Though Leonie liked the Continent, and
liked America and the West Indies, as far
as scenery and climate were concerned, England was the country whose moral and intellectual atmosphere really suited her. She
felt here a " *bien-étre* " that she experienced
nowhere else. And her work among the
tenantry was pleasant to her. She liked dif-

ficulties, and here she found plenty, some
in herself, and some in her people. But
they were difficulties frankly and fearlessly
faced and fought with, and one by one over-
come. After many efforts, and much time
lost in fruitless attempts, fruitless because
ill-directed, she found she could understand
the poor, and make them like her. This
grand fact discovered, nothing discouraged
her for long. There might be failures, dis-
appointments, trials, and vexations enough
and to spare, but after each she returned
again to the charge with fresh and unconquerable spirit and energy, having well learnt
not to

" *   *   * bate one jot of heart or hope,
But still bear up, and steer right onwards,"

not looking for any reward here, knowing that
life is but

"   *   * a little strife, where victory is vain,
Where those who conquer do not win, nor those
    receive who gain."

"Leonie, come here, I want to talk to
you," said Lord Bournemouth to his wife,
as she returned from the village one morning.

" About those letters? What a quantity you have!" she said. "Is this long one from Arthur?"

"Yes—but you can read that by-and-bye. He talks of being able to come home next year, but says it is very uncertain. That, however, we must not mind, for he is getting on capitally, and says there is every chance of his being able to get his majority soon. Fortunately the money is ready. But it was about these other letters that I wanted to consult you."

" Some more candidates for the living, I suppose," returned Leonie. "The modesty of some of these good gentlemen is really remarkable!"

"More candidates—I believe you! And not one who seems likely to suit. What a thing it is, having a living to fill up!"

"It is a much greater thing not having a living to fill up, especially if it happens to be already filled by a person you don't like," returned Leonie. "It is really providential, our old Rector's death happening just now; and when once the trouble of

selection is over, you will find you are
saved five hundred other ones. Now we
shall be able to have a Scripture Reader."

"The trouble of selection is worse than all
the other troubles put together. The more
I inquire, the less I seem likely to find what
I want. Now here is a letter from that
man who appeared so precisely the sort of
person to suit us."

" Well?"

"Well—he has thought it his duty to go
out as a missionary to India. I wish he
had thought it his duty to stay in as a
missionary at Avonbury!"

"It is a pity he has failed us," observed
Leonie. "But we have plenty of time; so,
if the other applicants don't seem likely to
suit—"

"And they don't," remarked Lord Bournemouth, in a parenthesis.

"I advise you to wait, and look about
you a little longer. Is that letter for me?
How came I not to have it before? I
suppose it was overlooked."

"There's Dorchester on the seal; who

can be writing to you from Dorchester?"
said Lord Bournemouth, as he handed her
the letter.

"The Duchess—what can she have to
say, I wonder? It is extremely difficult to
interpret her English," said Leonie, as she
read on. "The meaning of it is, as far as
I can gather it, that Dorchester does not
suit 'dear Anne' and the children, and she
wants to know if it could be managed that
they should come here."

"Freddy Fitzgermaine! How would it do,
Leonie?"

"There is not a word said about him,
but I suppose he knows what is going on,"
observed Leonie.

"I don't think he would object," said
Lord Bournemouth, "for he has always said
he should like a larger and less prosperous parish than Dorchester."

"Personally, I like the little I have seen of
Mr Fitzgermaine," said Leonie; "but there
are one or two objections. In the first place,
about Geraldine. I don't think it would be

advisable to renew an acquaintance with the Fitzgermaines." ·

"But this is only the cousin," said Lord Bournemouth; "and Fitzgermaine himself being on the Continent, and the thing so long blown over, I don't think that need stand in the way."

"Then I do not like his opinions," said Leonie; "I remember Geraldine found them rather troublesome in her poor husband's lifetime."

"But I assure you they are greatly modified now," said Lord Bournemouth eagerly. "And I hear his church is very well filled."

"That sounds well," said Leonie, "for ours is not, at present. But I won't answer the letter yet. We will take time to talk it over, and make inquiries."

"I shan't be in a hurry to settle," answered Lord Bournemouth, "for, to tell you the truth, the thought of having Freddy here is so particularly pleasant, that I am afraid of consulting my own inclinations too much."

"I shall not be led astray by any undue

preference for Lady Anne," said Leonie, with
a half serious face, "nor, I suspect, will Geraldine. Let us take Geraldine's sense about
the matter. I don't know any one who can
give us a better opinion in a case of this sort.
And here she comes."

Geraldine comes in, dressed in widow's
weeds, for her husband is dead, and she has
come to live with her brother and sister-in-law.
She looks pale, but placid and cheerful, and
less thin and worn than formerly. She is very
much of Lord Bournemouth's opinion, and
inclined to like the idea of Mr Fitzgermaine's
coming.

"He is very good," she said, "and has a
remarkable power of gaining influence over
men, which would be particularly useful here.
And I think, with Lindon, that he has greatly
modified his former opinions, only clinging to
a few trifling fancies concerning decoration,
and other externals."

"Well, I must sleep upon it," said Lord
Bournemouth, his specific in a doubtful case,
"and then we shall see. Where are you going
to, or coming from, Leonie?"

" I am coming from the village, and going back to it," said Leonie. " I must go to the Training School to-day. I am afraid it is not going on very satisfactorily."

" They very seldom do in England," said Geraldine. " Nothing is more wanted, and nothing more difficult to work. I know of one near Geneva which answers well; Gertrude had a nursery-maid from there; but in England the right sort of people don't send their children."

" I don't despair," said Leonie. " But I shall have to make some alterations in the plan, I think. Give up the self-supporting system, perhaps."

" Why, Leonie, I thought that was your pet theory," said Lord Bournemouth.

" So it was, but one has to give up one's pet theories now and then, and I would rather give up that than the school. If I lower the rate of admission, I shall lower the class of scholars, which is a pity; but then, on the other hand, I shall have more influence over the parents."

" The place from which Gertrude's maid

came was a sort of Home," said Geraldine, "the girls lived there entirely."

"I don't think that plan would do here; besides, I am doubtful of its being a good one. It is better to teach the girls to do their home duties well at home than to take them away from their families, which are, after all, the right Industrial Schools for them."

"There I agree with you," said Geraldine, "and I really do think some of the cottages look brighter and cleaner since the girls have been to your school. There are the Warners, for instance, but then they are in a new house."

"The Warners? I looked in there the other day," said Lord Bournemouth, "to see how your last new cottages answer, Leonie; and I must say I think them better than mine. Mrs Warner had just received a letter from their son in the —th, who, it appears, is getting on exceedingly well."

"I did not know he had enlisted," said Geraldine.

"It must have been a great trouble to them, for the poor always seem to consider it a positive disgrace if their sons enlist."

"So they do," said Lord Bournemouth, "more's the pity, for I could name one or two young gentlemen in this place whom we should be happy to spare to Her Majesty. Jack Warner enlisted by reason of pheasants. He joined a gang of London poachers who were obliging enough to undertake partly to supply the London market with my game;—a very different thing from a labourer's knocking over a hare or rabbit that has been feeding on his bit of ground; and a thing I couldn't stand. So I and my people went out one moony night when we heard our friends' guns pretty briskly at work in the plantations, and, after some trouble, we secured two of them and put the rest to flight. Jack Warner, who was the only countryman among them, after showing fight as long as a chance remained, took to his heels, and was not heard of for months, when I accidentally learnt that he had enlisted in the —th, which had since gone beyond seas. Our police were frantic at his escape, but I can't say that I was, for I saw no good in his retiring to jail for six months, to come out again a pest to the parish, in the shape of a confirmed

poacher; and he was cut out for a soldier, as
you would have said, if you could have seen
the judgment and pluck with which he
fought."

"And now that long story is finished," said
Leonie, "just listen to what I have to say. It
seems the boys' school is not going on well.
There are complaints about the master's
severity from the parents; groundless, I suppose, for the poor people are so foolish about
their children! And the curate complains—
probably with more truth—that the boys
don't learn as they ought to do, and that the
schools at Bristow are far more orderly, though
they are much larger."

"I'll look in there this afternoon, after I
come back from the Board," said Lord Bournemouth. "Who has been complaining? Give
me their names, and I will go and hear what
they have to say about it. It will be a thousand pities if the boys' school goes down, just
as it was getting on so well. As soon as our
new incumbent is regularly settled here, I
shall put it into his hands, for I don't understand the sort of thing myself."

" Don't be out later than five. There are those gentlemen you asked ; I have never even seen them before, so pray be in ; talking to people one does not know is so tiresome."

" What, the Bristow Infirmary Committee ? Oh, I'll be in ; you would find them horrid bores ; excellent men, all of them, but so stupid ! Well, never mind, you must put up with them to-night, and to-morrow your dear friend Sir James comes."

The result of Lord Bournemouth's sleeping on the Duchess' letter, was that he wrote to Mr Fitzgermaine and proposed his taking the living of Avonbury. It was not quite as good a one as Dorchester, as far as income was con-cerned, but the Fitzgermaines were tolerably well off, and did not mind the pecuniary loss. Mr Fitzgermaine was not sorry to leave Dor-chester, as he liked the idea of a larger parish, and very wisely considered that Lady Anne would be better further from her own home. And Lady Anne fancied herself and her chil-dren ill, and wanting " a change." So they moved to Avonbury, and a happy change it proved for all parties. Lord Bournemouth had

every reason to be satisfied with Mr Fitzgermaine, who combined the two excellencies so
seldom united in one person, of being a good
preacher, and a good parish priest. In the one
character he filled the church; in the other he
made himself universally popular among his
parishioners. As Geraldine had said, he had
a wonderful power of gaining influence over
men, which was the more astonishing as he
did not, at first-sight, give the idea of possessing enough strength of character to make any
great impression. He had dropped most of
his doctrinal extravagancies as he became
more clear in his views, and those that remained were modified to insignificance, when
set against the example of his real straightforward goodness.   As to his decorative
fancies, the villagers, puzzled and startled at
first, grew to like them for his sake, and were
especially pleased when he and Lord Bournemouth had a new organ put up in the church,
and, with Leonie's help, formed a regular choir,
the best choir in all the Vale, for Leonie well
knew how to select and teach her choristers,
and lead them with her own splendid soprano.

Lady Anne was at first amazed at Leonie's and Geraldine's regular system of parish work, then joined them, then found that she was pleased and interested, and finally left off her invalid habits one by one, and discovered that she was as strong as the rest of the world. She was as happy as the day was long, happier than any one else in Avonbury ; without her husband's morbid conscientiousness, Lord Bournemouth's and Leonie's harassing sense of responsibility, and Geraldine's worn and wearied mind. With employments that more than satisfied the demands of her somewhat narrow intellect, with Leonie to direct and support her, with pleasant society to fill up her leisure moments, she was happier than she had been at any time of her life. Her children found the benefit of mamma's increased health and strength, and were left less to the tender mercies of nurses and nursery-maids ; for Lady Anne was really fond of children when she could persuade herself that her nerves were strong enough to bear their noisiness. They were a fine intelligent little family ; and Geraldine passed

many a half-hour talking to them, and playing
with them when she met them in their walks,
or when she went to see Lady Anne at the
Rectory.

On one occasion she had gone there directly
after breakfast, with a message from Leonie to
Mr Fitzgermaine. He was out, and Lady
Anne up-stairs, so Geraldine sat down in the
drawing-room to wait for her. She had not
waited long before the door was violently and
suddenly thrown back upon its hinges, and
instead of the tall and stately presence of Lady
Anne, there entered a very small thin child,
with thick black curls down to her waist, great
shining, dusky eyes surrounded by black rings,
and a sharp and very white face. She was
not one of Mr Fitzgermaine's children, though
rather like them in some respects; but they
were stout, healthy, brown-and-red creatures,
with vigorous limbs and loud voices; besides,
Geraldine had just met them out walking with
their nurses, dressed in coarse brown holland
pinafores and thick leather boots; this child
wore a very bright pink silk frock, flounced and
frilled up to her waist, a gold necklace with a

large gold locket, gold bracelets, silk stockings, and little French bronze kid shoes.

"Where, I wonder, does she come from?"
thought Geraldine; "she looks as if she had
been used to walk on stilts at a country fair;
and yet she reminds me of some one I have
seen somewhere."

The mite—who hugged a costly and smartly-
dressed doll in her arms—walked up to her
without the slightest shyness, and said, in a
sweet and very distinct voice, and with a very
composed and assured manner, "What is your
name? Why do you come here?"

"I have come to see Lady Anne; do you
know where she is?"

"Aunt Anne is up-stairs; she is talking to
the cook about the poor people's soup; she will
come directly. The cook is a cross woman—
Aunt Anne seems afraid of her."

"What is your name?" said Geraldine,
highly amused.

"Lady Claribel Fitzgermaine."

"And your father's?"

"The Marquis of Fitzgermaine," was the
pompous answer.

· " Where do you live ? " inquired Geraldine.

" I live in Lancashire with grandpapa.   I
am staying here on a visit.   I don't like my
cousins—they make a noise, and wear such
ugly clothes.   Don't you think my clothes are
a great deal prettier ?   But perhaps you don't
know my cousins ? "

" I know them very well," said Geraldine.
" But you can't run about and play in that
smart frock ? "

" I don't run about and play ; that is for
children ; when I go out, I take a drive,"
replied the little Lady.

At this moment Lady Anne came in.

" Oh, my dear Geraldine," she said, " I am
so sorry to have kept you waiting, but really
Wilson was so tiresome about the list of poor
people for the soup ; and you know the time
is drawing near when it should begin.   She
would not let me put down the Smiths ; she
said the father was a drunkard, and the mother
a slattern, and the whole family rubbish."

" I hope you prevailed," said Geraldine.
" They are really very badly off."

" Oh, yes, I did ; but I had a great deal of

trouble about it, I can assure you. Clara, my dear," she continued, turning to the child, "take your doll, and go up to my maid. You can show her all its pretty clothes, and she will give you a bit of ribbon to trim its straw bonnet."

" I suppose you are going to talk about me to that person," said the child, marching off. Lady Anne and Geraldine looked at one another, and burst out laughing as she left the room.

"She is quite right," said Lady Anne. " My dear Geraldine, I don't know what to do about her, and want your advice. She is poor Clara's child, and lives with her grandfather and grandmother. They passed this place yesterday, on their way to pay a visit in Devonshire, and seemed rather encumbered by the little girl, as the lady they were going to visit does not like children, so I proposed that she should be left with me till they came back. You see how precocious she is ; the poor thing will be completely ruined if she continues to live with them ; they are spoiling her health and her character. They are bringing her up to be a beauty, just as young women in the middle classes are brought up to be governesses ;—it was the same with poor Clara. And her dress is so unsuitable ;—would you believe it? I looked over all her frocks, and could not find one plainer than that frightful pink silk thing! And they teach her to dance, and sing little songs before company! Where a Lancashire 'Squire can have picked up such ideas, I can't conceive—she is more like a little embryo French actress than anything else. I suspect the old aunt who brought out Clara has something to do with this little woman's education. She never goes for a walk, or even plays in the garden; they say she is not strong enough, and take her out in a close carriage."

"How old is she?" said Geraldine.

"Only five;—Freddy says she is the most precocious little wretch he ever saw. He is quite distressed, and says her godfathers and godmothers ought to interfere —but I don't know who they are; and, besides, god-parents never do interfere in these days. I wish they did; it would be far more in accordance with the meaning of our Church."

" It would only make mischief," said Geraldine; " no one would allow a godfather's interference. You would not like it yourself, if old Lord Somnolent told you that you were not bringing up Annie properly, and must alter your plan of education."

" Well, but, Geraldine, putting that aside, what am I to do about it ? "

" What do you think of doing ? "

" I should like to have her here,—at least for a long visit; but I don't suppose Mr Paget would allow it. It would be very difficult to manage. Shall I write to Fitzgermaine, who is at Vienna, and ask him if I may have her ? "

" You must settle it with Mr Paget first. It would not be fair to him to make any plan without his knowledge."

" It is hopeless to do anything with him, I am afraid. They are wrapped up in the child. And yet I really should not mind taking any trouble about it, though it is no business of mine, strictly speaking ; for poor Clara would

be miserable if she could see her. She will
die if they go on as they are doing now ; that
will be the end of it, I am certain."

" Is Lord Fitzgermaine fond of her ? "

" To tell the truth, I don't think he cares
much about her. He was very much disappointed that she was not a boy. And I should
not be surprised if that were the cause of their
bringing her up in this ridiculous way. They
know how much he thinks about beauty and
externals, and think that he will like her when
he comes back if he finds her pretty and accomplished. But they are quite mistaken in
what they are doing, for Fitzgermaine will
quite disapprove of her little second-rate arti-
ficial airs."

" Poor child ! " said Geraldine, " it is a
great pity, and they are spoiling her looks too.
I would really make an effort, if I were you.
Mr Paget must see that she looks wretchedly
ill ; and if you only propose it as a visit at
first, he can scarcely object to her visiting her
father's sister."

" No, that is true, and I hope to be able to
show him, when he comes back, that even a

week of real country life has done her good. I am going to take her out for a drive in the pony carriage this afternoon, for, thanks to them, she is really not strong enough to walk, and that will be better than a Clarence with all the windows shut."

" I hope you will be able to prevail on Mr Paget to let her stay," said Geraldine, "but don't be astonished if you find her a great trouble and worry."

"Oh, I am prepared for that—she is so unlike any child I have ever seen. And as to the responsibility; in any case she will be better off with me than with her grand-parents, and one can but do one's best."

" That is true," said Geraldine. " I wish I could take your common-sense view of things, but I can't help blaming myself if I plan a thing and after all it does not answer."

" It is tiresome certainly," said Lady Anne. " Has that happened to you lately ? "

" I have had a letter from my sister-in-law, Mrs Turnbull, this morning, to say that a governess I recommended her, and who has been with them for two years, is going to leave

them. And what makes it all the more pro-
voking is, that Miss Wood was a former governess of my own, for whom I was particularly anxious to provide well."

"And why doesn't she suit them?"

"She is not accomplished enough for the
eldest girl, and can't keep the little children in
order. But they told me, when they asked
me to recommend a governess, that they did
not care about accomplishments. And I am
sure that Miss Wood is quite equal to young
children, if the mother did not spoil them quite
so much."

"Does she mean to leave soon?"

"Yes, I believe so, and I should be glad if
I could hear of another situation for her. She
says she will try once again, but that if her
next place does not suit her she will give up
teaching."

"I wonder if she would suit me? I am
going to engage a governess for my little girls,
for they are getting quite beyond me. And if
I am to have Claribel it will be a good thing
that there should be a school-room where she
can play about while the others are doing their

lessons. She has been a great deal too much with nurses and old people. Will you inquire about it for me?"

"Certainly," said Geraldine. "But all this while I have forgotten my real business, which is to ask you to dinner to-day. Lindon wants to consult Mr Fitzgermaine about the boys' school. He has some ideas in his head about extending it, and introducing some of the higher branches of education, in order to fit the cleverest boys for something better than mere ploughmen, and would be glad to talk the plan over with him. And Leonie wants his advice about the Smiths."

"They give more trouble than all the rest of the parish put together!" sighed Lady Anne, in a very plaintive voice. "Yes, we will come with pleasure. Oh, what a blessing it is that I am not alone here, but have you and Lady Bournemouth to advise me."

"Aunt Anne, what ugly children yours are! Why do you dress them such objects?" inquired Claribel's solemn voice behind her.

She had come down unperceived, and was

watching her cousins, who were just returning from their walk.

"You should not ask such questions; they are not polite, especially for little girls."

"Wouldn't it be polite for you?"

"No, not at all; I should not think of making such remarks."

"Yes, you would; you said a little while ago that I was dressed unsuitably; and it is just as bad to be unsuitable as to be an object."

Lady Anne started. "How do you know I said so?"

"I heard you;—I was at the door. You talked a great deal about me, only I didn't quite understand it all; but I shall ask grand-papa. I shall ask him what a French—French —French actress means, and who Clara was, and why papa wished me to be a boy, and why he only likes pretty people. He will like me; I am pretty; but he will not like my cousins, and perhaps not you, for I don't think you're very pretty, nor is that person.

Why is she dressed in black, with that queer bonnet and cap on her head?"

"*Enfant terrible!*" murmured poor Lady Anne. "My dear, it is very wrong to listen at doors."

"But I always do it, Aunt Anne; or how should I know what people say of me? I should never have known I was pretty, only I heard grandmamma say so, when I was behind a door. Now I am going to meet my cousins. I hope I shan't catch cold. You need not be afraid to talk—I am really going."

And off she went.

"Oh, she must be a changeling!" exclaimed Lady Anne. "No mortal child of five years old could be so dreadfully precocious. Why, my little Annie could not speak plain till she was five;—and as to listening behind a door, and repeating all she heard!"

"You will have great trouble with her if you do take her," said Geraldine.

"I am prepared for that, and this very thing shows how necessary it is to separate her from her grand-parents. But I am afraid they will be dreadfully distressed at the idea."

Lady Anne found it no easy matter to put her charitable plans into execution. Mr and Mrs Paget were, as was to be expected, very difficult to persuade. But they could not but see that the child looked rosier and brighter for her week with her cousins, and set it down to the beneficial effects of Glastonshire air. They consented—and it was really very unselfish of them—to let her stay with her aunt for six months. Then Lord Fitzgermaine's consent had to be obtained. He wrote to say that it was all the same to him where the child was, but that Anne must not do anything against Mr Paget's wishes, as he had promised poor Clara before she died that the child should live with her mother's parents. So Lady Anne took this for consent, and kept her, and had some brown holland pinafores made for her like those her own children wore, and some stout country walking boots. The bracelets, silk stockings, and kid shoes were laid aside, though the locket was retained, as it was found to contain her mother's portrait.

Miss Wood was only too glad to leave the noisy Turnbull household, and come down to a quiet country parsonage, in the neighbour-hood of her dear Geraldine. And, on the whole, little Lady Claribel seemed in a fair way to improve, though she gave her unfortunate aunt an infinity of trouble, and, in some small particulars, corrupted her honest, simple-minded little cousins. She was a very quick child, being more like her father than her mother in that respect, and picked up many crumbs of knowledge while the children were at their lessons. Geraldine took a great interest in her, and often went up to the school-room to talk to her.

When the six months had expired, Mr Paget came, and carried her off to Lancashire. Both he and his wife were greatly pleased at her improved health and manners, and greatly distressed when, after she had been with them about a month, they perceived that she was going steadily backwards in both respects. Of course this was attributed to Lancashire air, so Mrs Paget wrote to Lady Anne, begging her to have the child for another six months, as the north certainly did not suit her as well as the south, but they hoped by that time her constitution would be more settled.

Lady Anne gladly consented, and back came Claribel to be re-reformed, having lost nearly all that she had previously gained at Avonbury, and having acquired nothing but a new stock of silk dresses and vanity.

Miss Wood rejoiced over her as over a lost sheep, and the little cousins, who had become used to " Clara's silly ways," welcomed her back joyfully.

CHAPTER III.

I deem'd that time, I deem'd that pride
   Had quench'd at length my early flame ;
Nor knew, till seated by thy side,
   My heart in all save hope the same.—BYRON.

IT was Miss Wood's plan, whenever the papers contained anything of particular interest concerning Lord Ernest Fitzgermaine, to read and expound the same to Claribel, who took it all in, in her usual precocious way, listened with her great eyes full of eager interest, and asked, whenever she saw a newspaper, "if it said anything about Uncle Ernest ?"

On one of these occasions, Claribel was
listening with wrapt attention to an account of
some daring feat of Lord Ernest's, and asking
a multitude of questions thereupon, which it
sometimes puzzled Miss Wood to answer.
" But how many soldiers had Uncle Ernest
with him ?"

" Two hundred and fifty."

" And how many were those wicked people?"

" I don't know, but many, many more than
that ; and if it had not been for Uncle Ernest's
prudence and foresight and courage, they
would all of them have been killed—every
one."

" What, all the two hundred and fifty men ?"

"Yes—certainly, all the two hundred and
fifty men, and perhaps many more."

" What is Uncle Ernest like ?" was the next
question.

" He is tall, and very good-looking, with
dark brown hair and moustaches, and has dark
blue eyes."

" Is he handsomer than papa ?"

" I don't know—some people think he is the
handsomest, and some people think Lord Fitz-

germaine is. Lord Fitzgermaine has dark hair and eyes, and a pale face like yours."

" Is papa as good as Uncle Ernest, and as brave ? "

This was rather a puzzling question, but Miss Wood answered circumspectly, " I don't know ; I don't know either of them very well ; but I suppose he is."

" Then why doesn't he go out and fight like Uncle Ernest ? "

" You wouldn't have a parson go out and fight blackies, would you, little one ? " said a man's voice behind her.

Miss Wood and Claribel turned round with start, and saw a middle-aged, high-bred-looking man, with a rather *roué* appearance. He was tall and very thin, and wore a white great-coat. Claribel asked her favourite questions, of which Lady Anne had never been able to cure her—" What is your name ? Why do you come here ? "

" To see your mother."

" She is dead," said Claribel, explicitly.

The gentleman, however, did not appear to hear; he had turned to Miss Wood, saying,

"I was told Lady Anne was out; but as I mean to take up my quarters here for some days, I came in, and looked over the house to see if anybody was at home. I hope I am not intruding here? This is the school-room, I suppose?"

"Oh, certainly—that is, certainly not—I am sure—Lady Anne will be in soon," said Miss Wood, in a nervous agitation directly.

Claribel, who did not know what nerves meant, turned round, and said with great self-possession, "Lady Anne will be happy to see you, I am sure. I am sorry she is out. Will you take a chair? We are reading;—we are reading about Uncle Ernest. I want to see him, and ask him all about those dreadful savages. I think he would answer me, for Miss Wood says he is very good-natured. Are you good-natured? Do you know him?"

"One question at a time, Mademoiselle, if you please. Of course I am good-natured;—and I know your uncle Ernest,—rather."

"Oh, do you like him? Do you think him brave and clever, as the paper does?"

"I suppose he is brave, and I dare say he

is clever. You see the paper thinks so, and
the paper tells us all what to think," said the
gentleman, with something like a sneer on his
thin lips.

Claribel looked intently at his face, and
evidently disliked it; she coloured a little,
and exclaimed abruptly, " I don't like you! I
don't like you at all, and I don't believe my
papa would like you;—he only likes pretty
people."

" Then he has taken a new line lately," said
the gentleman composedly, but rather surprised. " I'm afraid he brings you up to
think of nothing but looks; very reprehensible
in a parson's daughter."

" Parson's daughter! What do you mean?
My papa is not a parson, he is Lord Fitzgermaine, and I am Lady Claribel Fitzgermaine."

" Hallo! " cried Lord Fitzgermaine (for
our readers have doubtless recognised him),
facing sharply round, " you are Lady Claribel
Fitzgermaine, are you? "

He put up his eye-glass, surveyed her
leisurely, turned her round, still eyeing her
curiously, as if she were a little doll.

Claribel, who could not bear being touched, or in any way treated like a child, cried out peevishly, "Let me alone, I don't like you; you are rude and you are ugly."

"Hush, Claribel, hush!" said Miss Wood; "your aunt would be quite shocked!"

"So that is my daughter!" soliloquized Lord Fitzgermaine; "a nice piece of goods you are. Not altogether ugly, however, and really,—yes, really a little like poor Clara."

And so saying, he touched her lightly under the chin, as if to satisfy himself that she was really flesh and blood, and not wax. This was too much for Claribel; she struck out stoutly, crying, "Leave my chin alone! You ugly man! go away!"

"An extremely amiable daughter I have, really," said Lord Fitzgermaine, half to himself; "there, child, hold your tongue, do; I want to talk to this lady. Has Lady Claribel been here long?"

"Nearly a year, ten months that is, for one month she was with Mr Paget."

"Yes, I know that; and have you been teaching her all the time?"

" Only for the last four months."

"Does she learn well? Is she docile, good-tempered?" said Lord Fitzgermaine, quickly.

"Very, I have very little to complain of; and she learns still better with Lady Geraldine than with me."

" Lady Geraldine! What Lady Geraldine? Lord Bournemouth's sister?"

" Yes, she lives here, and she is very kind in teaching Claribel; she takes a great interest in her."

" Takes a great interest in her, does she? Come here, Claribel; you may speak now. Does Lady Geraldine ever talk to you about your father?"

" No, never; I talk to her about him sometimes, and ask her what he is like," said Claribel, rather sulkily.

" Oh—ay—and what does she say?"

" Mostly that she forgets. She doesn't say much about him, she knows Uncle Ernest best. But then, you know, she can learn things in the paper about Uncle Ernest."

" Ah—indeed; there, you may go, child; that's enough. How comes Lady Geraldine

to be so much here ? Where is her husband ? "
he continued, turning again to Miss Wood.

" He is dead, poor gentleman ; he died
about two years ago. A most happy release
for him and for her."

" Ah, I suppose so ; he was mad, was he
not ? or something of that sort ? And so she
is a widow ? "

And Lord Fitzgermaine, without waiting
for an answer, sat down before the table, rest-
ed his elbows on it, and his head on his hands,
and seemed lost in profound thought.

Miss Wood was a little astonished ; for he
was so much altered that she did not recognise
him, and wondered very much who this in-
quisitive and free-and-easy gentleman might
be. She was not sorry to hear a step approaching, which she knew to be Geraldine's.

Geraldine, on entering, was much surprised
to see the person we have described sitting in
the school-room, and apparently very much at
home. She did not recognise him, nor he her,
till Claribel started forward crying out, " Oh,
here you are, Lady Geraldine ! send this man

away—I am tired of him; he has asked such a quantity of questions, and a great many about you."

" Claribel! Claribel! you let your tongue go too fast!" said Miss Wood, with an imploring glance at Geraldine. She was a little puzzled; but Lord Fitzgermaine, who had risen directly she entered, addressed her with more politeness and ceremony than he had yet shown.

" I am afraid I must appear an intruder, Lady Geraldine, but I am waiting for my sister, Lady Anne. Perhaps she has come in ? "

" Not yet ; but she cannot be out much longer, I imagine," said Geraldine. " I suppose I am addressing Lord Fitzgermaine ? "

He was rather disappointed at finding her so composed; he had hoped that his sudden apparition would have had some effect upon her, but replied, " Yes ;—I am very much altered, I believe—and you also, if you will allow me to say so. I did not know you at first."

" Very probably. But I came, by Lady

Anne's request, to take Claribel out, if Miss Wood does not object, and I suppose I must refer to you also now?"

"Pray don't;—I hate responsibility;—I have no wish at all to interfere with her management; it seems to be answering extremely well," he said, very coldly.

Geraldine was vexed with his manner; she thought it unkind to the child, who had been looking forward with great pleasure to seeing her father at some future period. Claribel now for the first time began to comprehend who he was, and exclaimed with a look of great consternation, "Oh, is he my father? Oh, I don't like him! Send him away, Lady Geraldine, he is not at all what I expected. I can't bear his ugly face, and his great white teeth, and his frightful white coat. I don't want him, he is not agreeable."

"You must not be angry," whispered Geraldine reproachfully, noticing the very unpleasant expression of Lord Fitzgermaine's face; "remember what a child she is; and apparently you have done nothing to conciliate her. She is inclined to be very fond of you."

" She takes an extraordinary way of showing
it," said Lord Fitzgermaine, coldly. " There,
Claribel, let's have none of this. We shall get
on well enough in time, I dare say. Go with
Lady Geraldine, if she is good enough to be
bored with you,—I suspect she is the best
friend you have."

" Aunt Anne is the best friend I have, and
then Uncle Frederick, and grandpapa and
grandmamma, and then Lady Geraldine—and
I don't think you're a friend at all. But perhaps I shall like you by-and-bye—I shall try
to do so."

Lord Fitzgermaine burst out laughing.

" Very well," he said, " that will do. There,
off with you—I've seen enough of you for the
present."

Geraldine was sorry for the child, but Claribel
did not seem much hurt ; her feelings were not
very sensitive, and she was too young to have
made any romances about papa. She walked up
to him, and held out her hand, saying, " As you
are my papa, I shall shake hands with you now ;
by-and-bye, if I like you, I shall kiss you." And
just touching his hand lightly with hers, she

gave a little nod, and walked out of the room, followed by Geraldine. It happened to be the best thing she could have done. Lord Fitz-germaine was immensely amused at her pre-cocity, and the cool assurance of her man-ners; besides, her sweet cold voice reminded him forcibly of her mother, of whom he had been really fond, after his fashion. He turned to Miss Wood, with a more amiable expression of face than he had yet assumed, and said, " Really your pupil does you credit ;—she is very forward for her age, is she not ? I think she will be pretty, not as handsome as her mother; but that's scarcely to be expected. It is very kind of Lady Geraldine to be troubled with her; is she fond of all children, or only of Claribel ? "

" Lady Geraldine is very fond of all children ; she takes a great deal of notice of Claribel, but so she does of her cousins."

"Oh—ay. Do you think her like me? " was the next somewhat inconsequent question.

Considering what trifling things generally threw Miss Wood off her balance, she answer-

ed with tolerable composure, " Like your
Lordship? Indeed, you must excuse me—
I scarcely know; certainly she is dark and
pale."

" Yes—yes—I know all that—but does
she look like me—does she speak like me;
does Anne ever say she reminds her of me ? "

" I believe not ; indeed I have sometimes heard Lady Anne say that her eyes
and voice are strikingly like the late Lady
Fitzgermaine's."

", That's not true," said Lord Fitzgermaine quickly ; " her voice is like her
mother's, but her eyes are not; her mother's
were very soft, and this creature's are bright
and sharp."

" I believe, now I think of it," said Miss
Wood, " that Lady Geraldine once said,
talking to Lady Anne on the subject, that
her eyes were more like your Lordship's
than Lady Fitzgermaine's."

" Ah—indeed—Lady Geraldine said that,·
did she? " said Lord Fitzgermaine, looking
very much pleased. " And so Lady Gerald-

ine lives at the Castle? Does she often come here, or does Anne often go there? Is there much intercourse between them?"

"A great deal; they see one another constantly; sometimes two or three times a day."

"Does Lady Geraldine go out much in the village? She used to be fond of poking about among cottages?"

Miss Wood looked rather hurt at this expression, and replied with dignity, "Lady Geraldine goes constantly among the poor people; there is no one more charitable than she is, not even Lady Anne or Lady Bournemouth; the people often tell me that she is like an angel from heaven."

"That's true, at any rate," said Lord Fitzgermaine with emphasis.

"You know her very well, I presume?"

"Oh, yes—that is, I did; but every one knows how good she is."

"Indeed she is," said Miss Wood, warming up. "I don't think there is any one in the world as thoroughly and consistently good as she is. I ought to know, for I educated her—I was her governess. And what an admirable wife she made to that poor unfortunate man; for unfortunate one must consider him, notwithstanding all his wickedness."

"Wickedness, how so?" said Lord Fitzgermaine.

"Oh, his deluding the poor child into running away with him before she was old enough to know her own mind; and then latterly he treated her shockingly."

"Did he?" exclaimed Lord Fitzgermaine. "Brute! What was the cause of that?"

"I don't know, for nothing could be more devoted than her conduct to him. It may have been insanity coming on; so perhaps he is more to be pitied than blamed for it. But you must have seen a great deal of them when they were at Dorchester, my Lord? You must have observed all this?"

"Oh, ah, was it then that you mean? Yes, certainly;—we all thought he didn't behave well to her, but it was nothing very striking. Perhaps he was worse at home than when with us, though."

" I believe, to speak more correctly, it was after they left Dorchester that his conduct became really almost unbearable. She suffered a great deal at that time ; and then she lost her sweet little girl."

" Oh, the child is dead, poor thing, is it ? Well, it's all for the best, I dare say ; you know insanity is apt to run in families. And she is on good terms with her brother ? "

" The best possible. Lord Bournemouth is fonder of her than of any one in the world, except his wife. They are a most united family ; I don't know two sisters-in-law who agree so well together as they do."

" Indeed ? That's Lady Geraldine's doing, I suppose ; I don't fancy that Lady Bournemouth is a very amiable person."

" Oh, indeed she is," said Miss Wood, quickly ; " she is an excellent person, and so clever ; such an agreeable companion for

dear Lady Geraldine. They are always together, and place the most perfect confidence
in one another."

Somehow this did not seem to please
Lord Fitzgermaine ; however, he continued,
" And Lord Bournemouth? Didn't I hear
that he has gone to the good, or something
of the sort ? "

" Lord Bournemouth is truly good; he
is a model for all young noblemen," said
Miss Wood, stiffly.

" Oh—I dare say—I hate model men,"
said Lord Fitzgermaine, with a yawn. " Here
comes Lady Anne. Good morning—Miss—
Miss—I'm much obliged to you; these details
have interested me greatly."

He bowed civilly, and left the room,
leaving Miss Wood feeling rather uncomfortable, and fearing that she had talked
too freely of the family; but whenever she
began the subject, it was one she did not
easily drop. Of course she was entirely
ignorant of all that had previously passed
between Geraldine and Lord Fitzgermaine,

or she would never have suffered her name to pass her lips.

Lord Fitzgermaine, having learnt all he could from her, sauntered down to meet his sister, with an outward appearance of great unconcern, but inwardly rather doubtful of his reception. Poor Lady Anne's consternation may be imagined when she saw her brother advancing to meet her, and heard him say, "Well, Anne, how are you?" just as if they had only parted the day before.

"Fitzgermaine!" she exclaimed. "Oh, how came you here? You are not going to stay?"

"Really you are very hospitable! Yes, I am going to stay, if you can put me up. Where's Fred? Perhaps he will be more gracious than you are."

"Indeed he will not," said Lady Anne. "You ought not to have come. You know that Geraldine Lawrance is at the Castle."

"I did not know it till I came here, and now I am here, I shall certainly not go away. I suppose Bournemouth didn't have you here on condition that you should never see me?" he said, with something like a sneer.

"Of course it was not put into words, but it was a very well understood thing that we should not have you here," said Lady Anne.

"Oh, come—I can't have all this nonsense," said Lord Fitzgermaine, impatiently. "You have vegetated in the country till all your ideas have grown rusty. The thing is all over—and, after all, I did no more than hundreds of other men, of whom no one thinks the worse for it."

"Ask Lord Bournemouth his opinion," said Lady Anne. "And if my ideas are rusty, you will find Frederick's are equally so."

"What absurd twaddle! You have grown a regular Methodist. I did her no harm; I dare say she rather liked the excitement."

"You behaved shamefully!" cried out Lady Anne. "You made her miserable—you made her wretched husband ill-treat her—you damaged her character, and escaped all the blame yourself. If you were not my brother, I would never see your face again."

"Nonsense—don't make such a fuss," said Lord Fitzgermaine, frowning slightly, and evidently uncomfortable. "Are you going to dine at the Castle soon? I suppose you go there pretty often?"

"We are going to dine there to-night."

"Then I shall go with you. It's a long time since I've seen the Bournemouths—"

"You will do no such thing," interrupted Lady Anne. "I should not dare to look Lord Bournemouth in the face, if you came with me."

"You must settle that as you please—I shall go," said Lord Fitzgermaine, doggedly.

"You will not," said Lady Anne firmly. "Neither I nor Frederick will allow it."

"As to Frederick, I shall soon manage him, if I know him; and I suppose you won't oppose your husband," said Lord Fitzgermaine, contemptuously. "So we will let it rest till he comes in. And I ought not to quarrel with you, for I am really very much obliged to

you for the trouble you have taken about my
brat. I can easily fancy that those twaddling
old people were spoiling her;—they brought
up poor Clara in such a fashion as never was,
until I took her in hand."

" Claribel will be more clever than her
mother, and just as sweet-tempered and amiable," said Lady Anne. " You must learn to
like her, Fitzgermaine, she is really a very nice
child."

" Oh, yes—I dare say—I'll take it all on
trust. However, she seems to have her wits
about her. I found her listening to the
despatches as if she understood all about
it."

" Oh, are they not delightful? " said Lady
Anne. " Ernest's is so well written—so clear
and straightforward. And you can have no
idea how highly every one in England thinks
of him. Dear Ernest! how I should like to
see him! "

" Ah! yes—he is quite the rage now. We
shall have all the girls collecting bits of his
hair, and writing to him for his autograph

when he comes home. I dare say you don't think me worthy to be his brother."

" I don't," said Lady Anne bluntly. "However, it is honour enough to have one brother like him."

"If I was not a very amiable character," observed Lord Fitzgermaine, "you might make me jealous of him. But I seem to feel very well contented to be as I am, and let him be as he is."

" At least, then, you need not make a boast of it," said Lady Anne. " Here is Frederick. You may settle your matters with him—if you can."

She left the room, and Lord Fitzgermaine waited in some uneasiness for his brother-in-law's entrance, though he had no doubt of being able to bully the mild-tempered Freddy into compliance. He was mistaken however. Frederick's manner was less blunt than Lady Anne's, but he showed very plainly that Lord Fitzgermaine was the last person he wished to see in his house; and when the question of the dinner party was mooted, he gave a very firm and decided refusal.

" I am astonished that you can propose such a thing. It would be against the commonest rules of propriety, and Lord Bournemouth is not a man lightly to overlook such an offence."

" Oh, that is the reason of your wonderful resolution ? " sneered Lord Fitzgermaine. " You are more afraid of him than of me."

Frederick Fitzgermaine's pale face flushed, and his eyes sparkled, but after a few moments' silence he answered quietly, and without taking any notice of the last remark, " You will not go to the Castle with us, and you will only stay in my house on the distinct understanding that you do not at any time intrude yourself on Lord Bournemouth, or any of his family, without a special invitation."

" Which, I suppose, you think I may whistle for ? "

" I don't know how Lord Bournemouth may think it proper to act; I know what I should do if I were in his place," returned Mr Fitzgermaine. " However, on the conditions I have named you may stay here as long as you like. I leave it to you to decide how long that shall be, but I must say that the shorter it is the better I shall be pleased."

"Well, you are at any rate straightforward, and really I like you all the better for it," said Lord Fitzgermaine, whose feelings, like his daughter's, were rather of the toughest.

He thought over all his chances and opportunities.

"I can't get into the Castle, that's certain; and all the better too, perhaps. I shall have plenty of occasions of seeing her in the village without that Bournemouth woman—confound her! I don't think I should quite like to face those great black eyes of hers. Bournemouth himself is not altogether pleasant when put out; though I would rather have him to do with than his wife, any day; I can't stand a woman. Let me see, I must not stay here for more than a week, I suppose; Fred might advise himself to turn me out of doors, the fellow has plucked up such a spirit. A good deal may be done in a week, especially with the child as a go-between; really, Fortune seems to favour me; Geraldine may be Lady Fitzgermaine yet; I dare say she will be glad enough of the chance. Your good people always marry better than any body else. I might make a better marriage, my first was nothing particular; however, I can afford to please myself; and it is worth while to patch up matters with the Bournemouths. And then of course the child will live with us; she seems an amusing monkey, and I rather like sharp children. Yes, it will suit very well; and really, if all that governess said is true, I got her into a deuce of a scrape, and owe her some reparation. She is not a beauty; but I married a beauty once, and it didn't answer in some respects; she was a dear, good creature, but she bored me; one can't have everything. Hallo! there is Geraldine and my brat; suppose we begin at once." He went up to them and said, " Well, Claribel, have you had a pleasant walk? But of course you have."

" Yes, of course," said Claribel. " I always have pleasant walks with Lady Geraldine; she tells me such beautiful stories. Perhaps she will tell them to you if you ask her."

" You ask her for me," said Lord Fitzgermaine.

" No, I shan't ; you can ask for yourself ; it's silly to be shy ; Aunt Anne always tells Annie so."

" She has no reason to tell you so, I suspect," said Lord Fitzgermaine, laughing.

" No, indeed ; sometimes she says I am too forward.   But let us sit down on that bench ; I am tired."

" I am going home, Clara," said Geraldine ; " I shall leave you with your father ; mind you are good, and do what he tells you."

" I am sorry to drive you away," said Lord Fitzgermaine in a low tone ; " my little girl will probably find more pleasure in your society than in mine.   I wish you good morning."

And with a slight bow he moved away, but Claribel ran after him, saying, " Come back, papa, I don't mind you now ; you may come back, and I am sure Lady Geraldine will tell you the story of Beauty and the Beast, if you are good."

" I don't think so, Claribel," said Lord Fitzgermaine, stopping, " but I'll come back and see, if you like."

" That's right ; if she won't tell you a story,

she will talk to you : why don't you talk to him ? " she said, touching Geraldine's glove.

" I have nothing to say," was the answer.

" Then why don't you talk to her, papa ?. You have something to say ; you have been to strange countries, and seen strange men and beasts. Why did you go ? "

" To see the men and beasts ; is not that reason enough ? "

" Then why did you come back ? Because you had seen them all ? "

" Because I had something to do in England."

" What was that ? Have you done it ? "

" Not yet."

" Shall you do it ? "

" Perhaps I shall try."

" That's right ; Uncle Frederick always tells me to try. When you have done it, will you come and live here with us ? "

" I think not ;—the house is too small for me."

" But could you not live with Lady Geraldine and Lord Bournemouth, and come here every day? I dare say she would be pleased to have you."

" I don't think so; why do you?"

" Oh, because you are Uncle Ernest's brother, and she likes Uncle Ernest, and I don't think she dislikes you; at least, I never heard her say she did."

Lord Fitzgermaine stole a glance at Geraldine, to see if she confirmed this opinion, but she was looking straight at the distant view, and did not seem to hear what was going on.

" People don't always say when they dislike a person," he observed.

" She does, mostly.   But there are very few people she dislikes, I guess."

" You little American !   Don't let me hear you use that word again ; I am sick of it," said Lord Fitzgermaine.

" It's a good word," was the answer, " and if Lady Geraldine does not say anything, why should you ?   She seldom scolds—never, that is ; I wish she were my mamma ; don't you think it would be a good plan, papa ? "

" Really, Claribel, I think it would," said Lord Fitzgermaine, smiling.

Geraldine saw the smile; it was not a
pleasant one, and offended her.   She rose to go.

" I am sorry the child's nonsense should
drive you away," he said; " surely you attach
no importance to it ? "

" Not to her nonsense, of course," said Geraldine, in great displeasure.

" There, Claribel," he said, " you have
talked too much; you are driving Lady Geraldine away; make your peace with her, and
hold your tongue."

" Oh, Lady Geraldine! you are not angry ? "
exclaimed Claribel in distress.   " What did I
say ?   That I wished you were my mamma ?
Was it wrong ?   Oh, I am sorry.   But I only
meant it in fun ; — you can't be my mamma ;
—she is in the pit."

" I am not in the least angry, Clara," said
Geraldine, determined not to be beguiled into
staying any longer, "but it is time for me to
go home."

She left them, and Lord Fitzgermaine felt
that he had lost his opportunity.

" There, go away, child," he said testily.
" I've had quite enough of you."

From this time he could never find an occasion of seeing Geraldine alone. It may easily be believed that he was never asked to the Castle, and Geraldine took good care not to stir out of the grounds unless Leonie or Lord Bournemouth were with her. He watched her, and dogged her steps, and crossed her path continually, but without success. The week was drawing to an end, and his sister and brother-in-law had both given him unequivocal hints that they did not expect him to prolong his visit beyond it. He grew desperate, for the more he saw of her the more his old passion revived, and he determined at all events to propose, not doubting that he should be accepted. He sometimes thought of writing, and actually made several beginnings of a letter, but could never finish it to his mind. Besides, he had always been readier at talking than at writing, and it is proverbially better to speak on these occasions.

Fortune at last favoured him. One day Leonie had a bad cold, and could not go out; Lord Bournemouth had gone to a meeting of the Board of Guardians; and a dying woman in one of the furthest cottages of the village sent for Geraldine to come and see her. Of course she went; Lord Fitzgermaine saw her go in, waited patiently for more than an hour till she came out, and then joined her. She answered all his questions in monosyllables, and at last, finding him determined not to leave her, told him pretty plainly that she did not wish for his society.

"I can't pretend to misunderstand you," he said, "and I would not venture to act in any way contrary to your wishes, but that I have something of importance to say to you."

"Well?" said Geraldine, vexed, yet feeling it necessary to hear him.

"I have long loved you, you know how well," he began.

She would have liked to cut him short at once, but she was afraid of refusing him before he had actually proposed, as he was just the man to turn round upon her, and deny having meant to do so at all. She exclaimed in a tone of repressed indignation, "You dare to say this to me!"

"I do dare," he said. "I dare to repeat it, and to say that I love you still."

"You insulted me once," said Geraldine, with a trembling voice, "take care how you do so again. Remember, I am differently circumstanced now."

"You had a husband then;—you have none now; and for that very reason there is no insult in my saying that I love you."

"I wonder that you can allude to that time," said Geraldine. "I should have thought that you would have been too glad to forget it."

"Forget it! can I ever forget the deplorable folly of which my love for you caused me to be guilty?"

"Folly! is that your term for the wickedness which made my married life miserable? And you are not ashamed to tell me that you loved me,—loved me when I was another man's wife."

"I loved you dearly; which all I suffered and all I lost for you may serve to show."

"You suffered nothing, you lost nothing!" exclaimed Geraldine. "It was I who bore all the blame—it was my character that suffered. But I do not know why you speak of this; certainly you have no right to do so."

"I have, Geraldine, for I would now offer you the only reparation in my power. Will you marry me?"

"Marry *you!* Thank Heaven, I have no need of reparation. We have said enough of this; my refusal is final. I do not know what makes you do this; unless you are much altered, no good motive."

"Indeed, I must say more. I have not fairly represented my feelings. Geraldine, I can give you love—true, deep love; I can give you ample means of carrying out your charitable plans; I can give you,—not a daughter to replace your lost one; I will not insult your grief by saying so,—but one whom I think you love. Geraldine, for her sake, if not for mine, will you not listen to me?"

"Your daughter is in no want of my care; Lady Anne is a mother to her," said Geraldine, coldly.

"But not such a mother as you would be. Geraldine, can you leave that poor child; can

you abandon me, when to both of us you
would be such a blessing? Has not Providence appointed these duties for you?"

"Pray do not talk of Providence," exclaimed
Geraldine, in involuntary horror. "I cannot
bear to hear you; for I know you do not
believe in it."

His face fell before the gaze of her pure eyes;
he looked guilty, as a man detected in a lie.

"Lord Fitzgermaine," continued Geraldine,
after a pause, "I have heard you to the end;
now listen to me. You talk of my being a
blessing to you; but you have destroyed your
own chance of possessing me. I will confess
that, had you restrained your feelings during
my husband's life-time, I might probably
have accepted you now; for there was a time
when I thought well of you. I have been
preserved from that delusion, for I doubt not
I should have been unhappy with you. You
talk of your child, you ask me to marry you
for her sake; Heaven forbid that I should do
evil that good may come of it. I know
that many women have been beguiled into
wrong and foolish marriages because they

could not see the plain path in a question of this sort; I thank God that I do, and that however skilfully you may urge your suit I can see what is His will and my duty. And now I have finished. Of course you see that this is final—there is nothing more to be said."

"Of course ;—I am very much disappointed, but if these are your feelings you are quite right to act as you have done. Good morning."

And he walked rapidly away.

"I am glad that is over," thought Geraldine. "I knew it was coming. Now, will Lindon be very angry?"

She went to the house, and found him in Leonie's room. Leonie looked flushed, and her breathing was rather hard.

"How are you, dear Leonie?" she said.

"Better, thank you; but I shall not be able to go out to-morrow ;—Lindon must keep guard over you."

"There is no more need," said Geraldine shyly.

"No more need? What do you mean? Has he gone?" exclaimed Lord Bournemouth.

" He has proposed," said Leonie.

"Nonsense!" said Lord Bournemouth. " Geraldine, has he ?   Have you accepted him?"

" He has proposed; — what should you think if I had accepted him ?"

" Think ?—that people must please themselves," said Lord Bournemouth, shortly.

" You need not be afraid; I have refused him most decidedly."

" That's right !   Then you will always live with us ?   You won't marry any one else?"

" Lindon, how selfish !" said his wife. " She shall marry any one she pleases."

" Or can," laughed Geraldine. " I shall never have the option of marrying again. God willing, I will always live with you."

" Thank you. And what did he say? How did he begin ?"

"Lindon, you are indiscreet," said Leonie. " How can she repeat all his fine speeches ? *Elle ne saura comment s'y prendre, pauvre mignonne.*"

" There is your French coming out again," said Lord Bournemouth; " where has it gone

all this while?   I like your mixture of French
and English."

" I left it off when I was so much with
your father in London ; he could not bear it,
so I took some pains to break myself of it.
But to return to Geraldine.   Any little particulars you can give us we shall be happy to
hear."

" I can give you no particulars," said Geraldine, " it was much like other matters of the
kind, I suppose.   I believe widowers generally
urge the claims of their first family."

" Oh, that was it?   Lady Claribel was to
be the inducement?   How could you resist
such a tempting bait ? "

" By answering that she is already provided
with a mother in the person of Lady Anne."

" And then ? "

" And then he replied that I should be a
better one, and that Providence had placed
me in the way of marrying him and taking
care of Claribel."

" Well," said Lord Bournemouth, " we know
that the Devil could quote Scripture ; so I

suppose Fitzgermaine can talk of Providence."

" I did not precisely tell him that; but I begged him not to do so again.   And instead —I did not quote Scripture, but I told him plainly my opinion, and that there was no more to be said on the subject."

"Like a true woman, you had the last word."

" Not quite; for he went off saying he was very much disappointed."

"So much for him," said Lord Bournemouth.   " He will go away now, I suppose ; probably to marry some one else.   I hope she will be a nice person, for that poor child's sake."

" I think he will marry a foreigner," said Leonie.   " Lord Ernest told me once that he admired a Countess von Fürstenberg — I think it was ;—an Austrian, and very handsome."

" If she is kind to poor Claribel, it does not matter whether she is handsome or not," said Geraldine.

"No fear of that," returned Leonie. "Claribel is just the child to please a foreigner. The only danger will be that she will be completely spoiled."

"I am going down to have a cigar," observed Lord Lindon; "Geraldine, are you going to stay with Leonie?"

"Yes, certainly; as yet, I have scarcely seen her all day."

"So this is over at last!" said Leonie, as her husband left the room.

"What is over?"

"This proposal; I have been expecting it ever since the child came; though I kept it to myself, for fear of annoying Lindon. And now you will really live with us, for I do not think you will marry any one else."

"Nor do I," said Geraldine, smiling. "Yes, as far as it depends on me, I can safely promise."

Leonie laid her head back on the cushions of her chair, closed her eyes, and whispered, "Lord, now lettest Thou Thy servant depart in peace."

Geraldine did not quite catch the words, but a sort of thrill went through her, and she said quickly, " What did you say, dear? "

" Nothing—nothing that I meant you to hear, at all events," said Leonie.

" How do you feel ?   Not worse, I hope ? "

" Not in the least ; rather better, if anything.   I shall be a great deal better when this oppression on my chest goes."

" Leonie, you will tell me if you are ill? "

" Yes, I will."

Geraldine was silent, but not satisfied. But the next morning Leonie was really better ; consequently Lord Bournemouth went out with his fishing-rod in extremely high spirits ; and Geraldine very cheerfully sat down by her, and began reading the papers to her.

" It is quite time for more despatches from the Cape to come," observed Leonie.   " They are due to-morrow.   I wonder if Arthur will be able to get leave.   When last we heard, everything seemed tending to peace, and if so, he might be able to come home.   How long it is since we have seen him ! "

" Five years," said Geraldine, " and that

makes an immense difference at his age. I do
wish he could come. If Lindon has nothing to
do, he might go to Bristow, and bring us to-
day's paper. I dare say he won't find the roads
so very hard."

"If he does, or is otherwise employed, I
will send for it," said Leonie. "He will be in
about luncheon time."

"He is coming in now," returned Geraldine; "he must have forgotten something—
probably his fishing-hook."

But Lord Bournemouth, instead of going to
his morning room, came up-stairs and opened
the door.

"Lindon," said Leonie, "are you inclined to go to Bristow this afternoon? We
want to-day's paper, to see if the despatches
from the Cape are out. They must have
come."

"They have come," returned Lord Bournemouth, gravely. "My dear Geraldine, I have
just met Freddy Fitzgermaine, and he tells me
Arthur is in England. He has brought the
despatches."

"Arthur is in England! how delightful!"

exclaimed Geraldine. "Just what we were talking about."

"If Arthur has brought the despatches, they contain something important," said Leonie, looking up quickly at her husband. "No bad news, I hope?"

"Indeed it is;—the war has broken out again, and Ernest Fitzgermaine is killed."

"*Mon Dieu!*" exclaimed Leonie.

"Poor Anne!" said Geraldine. "Oh, Lindon, is it quite certain? How did he know it? Is it in the papers?"

"It will be to-morrow. The War Office sent to the Duke, that he might not learn it first from the papers, and he telegraphed to Freddy. That is all I know, for the message was very short. Poor Lady Anne is perfectly wild with grief. Fitzgermaine went up to London last night to see his father. Freddy would have sent to us at once, but he made sure we should have heard it through Arthur."

"How dreadful!" said Geraldine. "Oh, I do pity Anne with all my heart, for she was so fond and so proud of him! And it is such a dreadful loss!"

" To them and to the country," said Lord Bournemouth, " for we have no one who can exactly supply his place there. Freddy and Lady Anne are going to Town as soon as she is a little more fit to travel —this afternoon, perhaps."

" I am sure the poor Duke and Duchess will want them," said Geraldine. " And about Arthur ? Where is he ? "

" I don't know, and I don't think it would be of any good for me to go up to London to meet him, for he will come down here as soon as he finds we are not there. And I don't like leaving Leonie till she is better."

" No," said Geraldine, " nor do I. And I suppose there will be nothing to keep him in London."

" Of course he must see the Duke," said Lord Bournemouth; " they will wish to have all particulars, and I dare say he has brought Ernest's things with him. But all that need only keep him a day. Probably the second post will bring a letter from him. At all events I shall go to Bristow on the chance, and get the papers."

CHAPTER IV.

Each in his own strict line we move,
And some find death ere they find love,
So far apart their lives are thrown
From the twin soul that halves their own.
                                        M. ARNOLD.

MEANWHILE Arthur had, after delivering his
despatches at the War Office, proceeded to his
brother's house, and finding it empty, took up
his abode in a hotel, meaning, as soon as his
business in London was finished, to go down
to Avonbury. His first care was to write to
the Duke, saying that he had some chests and
trunks of Lord Ernest's in his charge, and

begging to know into whose hands he should deliver them. This was in the evening, and then, knowing no one in London whom he cared to see, he had a solitary dinner at his hotel, and sat down to consider his plans. How changed everything seemed since he had gone out to the Cape five years before! though perhaps the change was more in himself than in any one else. He felt ten, fifteen years older for that short experience of real service; felt he had cast all the boy off, and was now completely a man, and a man with some knowledge of life, and power of using it. His prospects were good; he was, he well knew, considered a very promising officer; he had obtained his majority—the death vacancy going, as usual, in the regiment—though he would willingly have sacrificed that step, if by doing so he could have annulled the cause of it. His sorrow at Lord Ernest's death had been acute, and the coming to England, and having to give the account of it, and talk it over, had revived his first feelings of regret, as much as if it had happened yesterday. It was a satisfaction to find that Lord Ernest's loss appeared to be fully appreciated in England; the chief of the War Office had spoken of him in the highest terms, and mentioned the honours it had been in contemplation to bestow upon him, but for his untimely end. And every man Arthur knew who met him in the streets, stopped to talk about it, express his regrets, and lament the loss to the country, and the premature close of a life which was so valuable, and would have been so distinguished. And the laudatory leader which appeared in the " Times " next morning, and the laudatory speeches which were made in the House next session, were satisfactory; though, at present, these last not having yet taken place, Arthur could only think of them, and wonder if they would.

He next turned his mind to Avonbury;— he would go down there as soon as possible; he was sure old Lindon did not know where to find him, or else he would certainly have come to meet him. Arthur had always been on very good terms with his brother, notwithstanding the difference of age; it had begun in his early youth, for nothing impresses a little boy more than good-nature from any one many years his senior, and Lindon was good-natured to everybody. Lately Lord Bournemouth had become proud of his gallant young brother, as well as fond of him, seeing plainly that Arthur was capable of making some stir in the world, and would say with perfect acquiescence, "Arthur has three times my energy; and as to ambition, I think he has got my share as well as his own. His head-piece is good enough—never fear but he will do well."

He liked and admired Leonie, who liked him; and he was devoted to Geraldine. However depressed and lonely he might feel now, he well knew his welcome at Avonbury would make up for a good deal. About half past ten a note was brought to him from the Duke, begging him to come to Dorchester House at ten the next morning, if that hour suited him, as he and the Duchess were extremely anxious to hear all he had to communicate respecting their son.

Arthur of course complied, but he only saw Lord Fitzgermaine, who apologized for the

Duke's absence, saying that his father had
been completely worn out with the shock and
excitement, and had deputed him to receive
Major Vivian in his stead. They talked for
some time, very much against Arthur's will,
who found in Lord Fitzgermaine—despite his
real courtesy of manner — an indifference,
which surprised him, to the details he had to
relate.

"I will send to your hotel for my poor
brother's property this morning," said Lord
Fitzgermaine at the close of their interview.
"I understood you rightly that you leave town
to-day?"

"Not till to-morrow, at the soonest."

"Then I shall know where to find you in
case there is anything I wish to consult you
about. Good morning, Major Vivian; had we
met under less melancholy circumstances, I
should have been delighted to see more of
you; my brother wrote of you in such high
terms that I have always felt the greatest wish
to renew our old acquaintance; perhaps, if
you are in London later, you will let me
know?"

To this astounding piece of impertinence, Arthur replied by remarking coldly that his plans were entirely unformed, and took his leave.

" That's a good-looking fellow, and rather like Geraldine ; it makes me feel quite old to see him so much of a man. Well, I must send for these boxes at once; I hope my father will look over them himself; it is the sort of thing I don't half like."

The Duke, on being referred to, refused to open the trunks; he was heart-broken at the death of his favourite son, and felt he could not bear the sight of anything that had so lately been his ; therefore he desired his son to do it for him; Mr Fitzgermaine and Lady Anne not having yet arrived.

There was not much to look over ; Ernest had been very simple in his habits, and his possessions were extremely few ; some well-worn clothes, military and others ; some well-read books, mostly on history, with a few scientific, and a few on general subjects; and some miscellaneous articles, certainly more calculated for use than show. The only things that attracted Lord Fitzgermaine's attention were a bundle of letters, and a rough MS. book, apparently a journal.

"I dare say they are worth looking through," he thought. "Ernest used to write well. I have nothing to do this evening, and can glance over them before I give them to my father."

Accordingly that evening, after the family had separated for the night—Lady Anne and her husband had come, and the evening had been very short and very sad—he shut himself up in his room, and, lighting his candle-lamp, prepared to read.

The journal first claimed his attention; the entries were very short, but as it extended over a considerable time, it made a good-sized book. It began in those early days when Ernest was a young man about Town. All that was recorded in this part was the parties to which he had been, put down without any comment whatever, the horses he had bought and sold, a few inconsiderable losses at cards and billiards, a few trifling bets, and matters of that kind. At last there came this entry:

" *Went to Lady Bournemouth's ball ; danced once with Lady Geraldine.*"

"That's odd," thought Lord Fitzgermaine ; " I see he has not put down any of his other partners. Here it is again : ' *Went to Lady St Aubyn's, danced once with Lady Geraldine Vivian,*' and again. He never danced more than once in an evening with her, it seems ; she liked me the best in those days ; I used generally to dance with her twice at one party. What is this ?—' *Received an invitation to dinner, from Lady Bournemouth, written by Lady Geraldine. Threw over Beauvilliers, and went.*' Ernest must have had different tastes from mine then ; I used to think Beau gave the pleasantest dinners in London, and should certainly not have thrown him over for the Bournemouths. Here is her name again. By the bye, it strikes me now, could he have liked her ? All the best men in London did, and I dare say Ernest was not behindhand."

He ran his eye on through the book. Lord Fitzgermaine was not at all wanting in acuteness, and he presently became convinced that his brother had not only liked, but loved her to an extent he had never dreamt of in his own case. But when had the feeling died away? He hurried on; the journal became more diffuse; the events it recorded were no longer so frivolous; but what it did record was generally commented upon in a few short, vigorous sentences.

"Very good writing this," was Lord Fitzgermaine's next reflection; "that sentence is quite epigrammatic. Judgment good too; all he says about men and things is worth reading. Here he took up French; and he seems to have read a good deal; rather a stiff, practical style of book. It is a pity he couldn't talk about what he knew; he might have made more play if he had been readier with his tongue. Well, let me see; this is after she eloped; I suppose he gave her up then. No, by Jove, clearly he didn't; upon my word, I don't believe—now really I don't—that he ever forgot her, or cared for any one else. No, certainly not. What is this?"

Lord Fitzgermaine had now come to a part where his brother by a few hints indicated that, as we know, he had, before the elopement, only been waiting for some slight encourage-ment from her to propose. He laid down the book, and threw himself back in his chair.

" Now what a fool the girl was ! Here was a fine young fellow, for he was that, though one does get rather tired of Aristides the Just. Only waiting for encouragement, and she never saw that he liked her, and ran off with a snob of a tutor she did not care two straws about. Well, some women *are* blind ! "

He went on. The next part of the diary referred to regimental matters, and showed how from henceforth he had given himself up to mastering his profession, practically and theoretically. Lord Ernest was the last man in the world to condescend to vanities; but the simplest entries, the barest notification of facts, showed involuntarily how highly he was thought of in his regiment, how he was es-teemed by the elders, and liked by the youngers. " He appears to have been the general referee in disputed cases. Well, I know no man I would sooner have gone to in a difficulty; plenty of temper, good knowledge of the world, and sound common sense ; those are the right qualities for a 'third party.' Looked after his men well too ; the colonel seems to have had a good opinion of him, and Little was a fair judge of character. I shouldn't say he ever joined in the youngsters' larks ; it must be a great bore to be a rising anything. Ernest was not exactly a prig, but his notions were too strict for me on most subjects. And authorities had a way of making rather a fuss about him ; such men as Sir George Wharton, for instance ; quite unnecessary, for I dare say there are plenty in the army as good as he. I don't see the advantage of a paragon of a younger brother—or a paragon of any sort indeed. Well, it all goes on pretty much the same, only I can see symptoms of a steady rise ; and here he goes off to the Cape."

Here the diary became much more circumstantial ; evidently he had attained more clearness of thought and facility of expression, and the new scenes he was thrown amongst had stimulated him to more sustained efforts of narrative. During the voyage, probably for want of something to do, he had written a few remarks upon different books, with now and then an extract; these Lord Fitzgermaine read with an approving nod, and he was not a bad judge of such things. Afterwards the entries became more entirely professional; certain events were related with great minuteness of detail, apparently for after-reference; his own opinion on different cases was recorded clearly and shortly, and in the manner of a man who had been used to have his judgment deferred to. But through all this Lord Fitzgermaine could detect, by the faintest possible signs, a latent undefined hope that Geraldine might yet one day be his.

" Upon my word, I should have given it up by then; but Ernest was a very bull-dog for perseverance."

Then came the skirmish in which he had been wounded, the return to England, and the discovery of Mr Lawrance's madness and failing health. And here hope seemed to revive; for the first time he saw his object clearly before him, and determined on working steadily and systematically to gain it. He would be worthy of her; he would make a name which he should not be ashamed to ask her to share when the proper time came; and from henceforward he worked on cheerily, caring nothing for fatigue, labour, danger; anything was welcome that helped in raising him to a level with her. In the hour of his greatest triumph he never thought himself worthy of her, but at no moment did he despair; nor did he become in the least unmindful of his profession, even in its dullest details. It must not be supposed that he said much about her, only a few suggestive words here and there; the rest was almost exclusively military, and showed in the simplest and plainest manner how he had toiled and suffered, caring for all around him, and never for himself; how defeat had only been a fresh spur, and responsibility a stimulus; how he had devoted himself heart and soul to his profession, giving it time and thought, and energy of body and mind—in one word, all his powers. He could grasp the most comprehensive schemes, and remember the most trifling details, was as solicitous for the welfare of every one around him as if he had a personal interest in them, and shrunk from no hardships so that he could ease the burdens of others. And all this was to be gathered from the most unadorned statement of facts, the most straightforward record of events.

"By Jove! he was a fine fellow, and I don't wonder at their being mad about him!" exclaimed Lord Fitzgermaine to himself. "There's a pith and mettle in him; and I like this sort of frank confidence in others and in subordinates. That's always a sign of a strong, large mind in a man of his acuteness; it's your little folks, who are afraid of committing themselves, that can't afford to trust. Now all this part about Montgomerie—how generously and wisely he upheld him through all that business, when the poor fellow must have broken down but for Ernest's steady support. And the result confirms what I say."

This was a most unusual burst of enthusiasm for Lord Fitzgermaine, proving, among other things, that if his conduct at times went considerably out of the straight line, it was not from want of the power of discriminating between right and wrong. One entry really touched him. It referred to a letter of his own, and spoke of the pleasure with which it had been received. He remembered that letter quite well, for it was the only long one he had ever sent his brother. He had been staying in a country house;—the party was stupid, the day rainy, and, having nothing to do, he had felt impelled to sit down and write a long letter to Lord Ernest. He wrote well and amusingly; the letter was full of news and of family gossip, and concluded, for him, quite warmly. And Lord Ernest had read it with such pleasure, and kept it so carefully!

"If I had only known it, I would have written oftener. I wish I had now, with all my heart."

Then came the news of Mr Lawrance's death; and the dream of his life seemed about to be realized. He had waited two years, and everything looked more and more promising— Geraldine at her brother's house, his own sister living at the gates, so that he should have every opportunity of seeing her; the Colony, settling down month by month. He might now, without the slightest prejudice to the

service, pay a visit to England, and try his
chance fairly. He applied for leave, and received it immediately, and was on the point of
starting, when suddenly the war broke out
again; Ernest, without a murmur, indefinitely
postponed his cherished plan, and, with cheerful alacrity, began all over again the work
that he had hoped was completely finished.

And then came the last battle—and then—
we know the rest.

"Poor Ernest!" said Lord Fitzgermaine.
He threw the book down, sprang up, and began pacing to and fro.

"I could offer her nothing like this—this
was what she wanted; no doubt she would
have married him. And I wish with all my
heart she had. I could have given her up to
him, for we were always good friends, ever
since the days when we were little fellows
together. He deserved her after all this waiting and working. Poor dear Ernest!"

He sat down, and looked at the letters.
First, carefully wrapped up, was that note of
invitation written by Geraldine, and mentioned
in the early part of the diary. There was a

bit of dried flower with it; probably something she had given him. Then came a short
letter from Lord Bournemouth ;—evidently
prized, because it contained a kind message
from her. Then a note from Arthur, enclosing
half a sheet torn off a letter of hers, relating
the arrangement that had been made about
Mr Fitzgermaine's taking the living of Avonbury. The rest were chiefly professional; one
was from Sir George Wharton, congratulating
him on his appointment to the command of a
district, and couched in the kindest and most
flattering terms.

" Really I am not astonished that he kept
that, though, Ernest was so shy of praise, it
would not have been wonderful if he had
burnt it as soon as he saw what it was."

And then there was his own letter, bearing
evident marks of having been frequently re-
read.

" This is all, and now let me tie them up
again. I wish the little goose could know
all she missed by that pretty elopement of hers
—her chance gone for the second time. She

would be sorry for it if she read this. Well,
and why should she not read it? Ernest would
like it, if he could know, I dare say, and so
should I; for it would pay her off nicely for
her cool refusal and spiteful speeches. Thank
Heaven she has not married me indeed! I
should just like to show her what a series of mis-
takes she made on the subject of matrimony.
Well, I'll do it. My father will never miss
them, for he knows nothing about them, and if
he sees these letters he will be quite satisfied; he
knows Ernest never kept papers in a general
way. She shall have the journal and all the
letters that relate to herself; and I should like
to see her reading them."

Lord Fitzgermaine immediately drew out
a sheet of paper, wrote a civil note to Arthur,
begging him to give the accompanying packet
of papers to Lady Geraldine, "as, after reading them, it appeared to him that such
had been his brother's wish — the papers
would explain themselves," packed the whole
up together, and sent them off the next
morning to Arthur, who, in due time, de-

livered them to Geraldine. Lord Fitzgermaine never knew whether they produced
the desired effect or not; the idea was good,
and he flattered himself that it had perfectly
succeeded. Whether it did or not, our
readers shall see.

CHAPTER V.

Old England still hath Heroes
  To wear her sword and shield!
We knew them not while near us,
  We know them in the field!

GERALD MASSEY.

Could you come back to me, Dougla, Dougla,
  In the old likeness that once I knew,
I would be faithful, so faithful and loving,
  Dougla, Dougla, tender and true!

    *   *   *   *   *

Oh, to call back the days that are not!
  Mine eyes were blinded, your words were few,
Could you know the truth now up in heaven,
  Dougla, Dougla, tender and true!

    *   *   *   *   *

ARTHUR, soon after the receipt of this packet, having finished his business in Lon-

don, went down by train to Bristow, the
Avonbury Station.   He felt in better spirits
than he had done since he landed; at
home he had nothing that was not pleasant
to expect; and he began to picture to himself how every one and everything would
look at the old place.   Perhaps Lindon
might meet him?   He had not 'written to
announce his arrival—Arthur was curiously
remiss about writing, except in cases of
absolute necessity — but still Lindon was
often at Bristow in the afternoon, and might
come up to the station on the chance.   Yes,
sure enough, there he was standing on the
platform, entirely unaltered — except in the
particular of having become rather stouter—
by the five years that had gone over him
since last the brothers met.   Arthur, for
his part, was so bronzed, so bearded and
moustached, so aged and developed, that
Lord Bournemouth actually stood opposite
to him without being in the least aware
who it was, till Arthur grasped his hand
saying, " Just the same as ever, I see ; don't
you know me?"

" Hallo, Arthur—is that you? No, indeed I didn't know you. Why did you not write? It is only a chance that brings me here; it struck me you might come to-day, so I just drove the phaeton in. Here, Robert,— put Captain Vivian's luggage in; there isn't much of it, I see. Now, Arthur, jump up."

" Major Vivian, if you please," said Arthur, climbing up. " Did you not see it in the Gazette?"

" No,— I must have missed it. How came that? The death vacancy, I suppose. Well, I congratulate you."

" Thank you ; — but I would willingly give my majority to bring back Ernest Fitzgermaine."

" I dare say ; but you see you can't; and Ernest could have made no better ending. I don't know when I have read anything I liked as well as his last despatch."

" I took it down from his dictation, when he lay dying."

" You must tell us about it when we get home; there was, as you know, some account in the paper; but not, I suppose,

half what you could tell us. Such as it
is, Leonie knows it by heart, I think."

"How is Leonie? In as good looks as
ever?"

"No—she has not been well lately"—
and Lord Bournemouth's handsome cheery
face assumed a graver expression, as he carefully disentangled a knot in his whip lash,
"she has had a bad cold. If it hadn't
been for that, we should have come up to
Town to meet you. Poor Geraldine must
have been disappointed at not going, but
she was good enough to say nothing about
it, and, for my life, I could not propose her
leaving Leonie."

"I am sorry she has been so ill; have you
been anxious about her?"

"No—I don't know that I have; but I become fidgety if she is the least ailing; you
would, too, if you had a Leonie. However,
she is all right now. You look flourishing, I
am glad to see."

"So I am," said Arthur; "and considerably more altered than you, I conclude. Are
the Fitzgermaines at Avonbury?"

"No—they went up to Town yesterday."

"Ah, that is right; I dare say Lady Anne would have wished to see me, and, upon my word, I don't think I could have faced it. Lindon, do you always drive that horse on the second bar?"

"Always," said Lord Bournemouth, with the grave conviction gentlemen are apt to entertain, that any question relating to their horses is of vital importance. He proceeded to give several weighty reasons for so doing, whereupon Arthur laughed and said, "I see an alteration now. You used not to be so ready with a reason, but I suppose you have given up that unparalleled laziness of mind and body in which you used to indulge."

"I'm not quicksilver now, if you mean that," said Lord Bournemouth, with a half laughing sigh, "and think of setting off in search of the Lotus when I have leisure. Tennyson's Lotus-Eaters must have been written for me; it would suit me precisely."

"I have read the thing you mean, I know, for Cherry once gave me a copy of Tennyson, but I can't have cared much about it, for it has quite gone out of my head.   There is a little volume of old ballads she gave me that I liked twice as well,"

"I suppose you couldn't take many books about with you?"

"One or two on mathematics, some stiff military gentlemen, a small 'Schiller,' for the sake of my German, and the volume I spoke of.   It is no use to take light books—one gets so tired of the very sight of them after they are read, so the ballads were the only things of that sort that went about with me.   And they were worth their room on the whole; 'Jamie Telfer,' and 'Kinmont Willie,' or 'Dick o' the Syde,' have given me many a ten minutes' amusement.   What a pretty thing that is on the hedge!   All this green English country seems like Paradise after the Cape; and yet I have brought some seeds for Cherry, which, if she succeeds in rearing, will, I dare say, make her wild to see the country they came from."

"I hope you've brought nothing danger-ously new or pretty in the way of plants; not for Geraldine's sake, but for Leonie's.   She is a will-o'-the-wisp for travelling, and a foreign flower always sets her longing to pick it where it grows. Not that she has been out of England since she first came here, I must confess."

" Why don't you take her abroad ? It would do her all the good in the world ;— quite set her up, if she isn't strong."

" My dear Arthur, how can you ask ? Here are all our improvements at Avonbury, which would come to a stand-still if we were away. It is not my choice, for nothing I like better than travelling. Now look there. Is not that an improvement ? I've cut down some trees at this turn, and let in a view of the house. It makes quite a fine figure from this part of the road."

" So it does," said Arthur ; " I did not think it could look so well from anywhere."

" When we come nearer, you will see where we have cleared a space for Leonie's flower garden. These are some of the new cottages, and that is the School. They don't look amiss, do they ? "

" No," said Arthur, wondering more and more at his brother's rural tastes, and the improvements he saw on every side. " You haven't lost your time, at any rate. I must not say another word about laziness. Ah, there is the flower garden, and there is Cherry walking in it."

" What it is to have young eyes, or indeed any eyes at all ! " said Lord Bournemouth. " Hold up, Maggie—you seem to be worse off in that respect than myself."

They were soon at the door, and Geraldine, with a start of delight, hurried to meet them as she saw Arthur sitting beside his brother. For the first half hour after they entered the house, she could scarcely take her eyes off him. She was so thankful to see him again, so anxious to hear all he had to say, so eager to find out if he were as altered in mind and character as in looks, that she talked and listened, till the dressing-bell rang, without a pause. She thought him very much changed, and certainly improved, and so he was ; and yet, though she did not at first discover it, he was, in many respects, very like the boy we first knew him;—like him in his brightness and care- less gaiety, in his somewhat sensitive disposition, and in his strong instinctive affection for herself. She could scarcely realize that a day had passed since she last saw him, he was so unchanged in his almost caressing manner, and the complete confidence he continued to give her. There was nothing of that cloud—one of the dreariest and saddest things in life—which often grows up between the fondest brothers and sisters when their paths diverge, and they begin to find separate interests and new affections; to know, without being able to understand it, that they cannot from henceforth be all in all to one another. Their place is filled up—theirs, which was the first of all! Well —better so. Some there have been who to the end were faithful to one another ;—some perhaps we have known — of some we have certainly read. Of this sort was Arthur. Neither wife nor friend could have come between him and Geraldine. Had he married, she would still have been his queen and star, and his wife must have been contented with affection, but not very warm love, or very great admiration. The wife had not yet come however, and there was nothing to damp Geraldine's pleasure in

finding her brother still unaltered, still all her
own.   She had perfect and complete delight
in his society, and sat enjoying it all the evening with a vivid pleasure she had not felt for
many a year.   The hours had never passed so
quickly, and when the time for separating
came, she went to her room with a heart so
light that the days of her girlhood seemed almost to have come back again.

She was up early the next morning, and
going down to the drawing-room, found Arthur
already there.

" Good morning," he said, " I am glad you
are early, for I have got into such early ways
that my appetite really won't wait.   When will
breakfast be ready ? "

" As soon as Leonie is down.   She is not
generally as early as I am, but to-day I heard
her singing like a lark in her room a full hour
ago, so I dare say she will not be long.   Does
not the old place look lovely in the morning
sun ? "

" There is no place like it," said Arthur.
" I have brought some flower seeds, which I
want to have planted on the south side of the

house, if Leonie has no objection; they will be just the right thing for it. Oh, and, by the bye, Cherry my darling, before I forget it, I have a parcel for you. It is some papers of Ernest Fitzgermaine's which were sent to Lord Fitzgermaine, who returned them to me, with a note begging me to give them to you, " as that had been his brother's wish."

" To me? My dearest Arthur, you must be mistaken; I have nothing to do with Lord Ernest's papers."

" It is Lord Fitzgermaine's mistake then, not mine. But I don't believe there is any, for his note was perfectly clear, and he said the papers would explain themselves. Don't open them now, for there is a good deal of it, and I want to talk to you."

Lord Bournemouth and Leonie had come in, and he, hearing Lord Ernest's name, said, " Ah, by the bye, Arthur, I meant to ask you more about Ernest. What an unfortunate thing his death was, coming just then!"

" Unfortunate! it's disastrous—losing our

best man now. There is no one to take his place."

" What did people think of him out there? As much as we did in England?"

"More, for no one else was thought of at all. He was so much the first that there was no second."

" How strange that he showed so little promise of superiority as a young man!" said Geraldine.

"You do him injustice there," said Leonie. "His intimate friends always recognised the superiority of his character, and the soundness of his judgment. And as to intellect, I think now, as I thought then, that his apparent dulness was chiefly a want of the power of expressing himself, added to a naturally slow development."

"I remember once," said Lord Bournemouth, " when we were at school together, there was a very deep fall of snow. As soon as it would bind, we made a Castle, regularly fortified; Ernest commanded the besiegers, and another fellow the garrison. To be sure, what fun it was! The snow lasted several days, and we had a regular siege. The garrison defended it stoutly, but at last a thaw threatened, and Ernest felt his honour was involved in taking the place before it became untenable. I needn't tell you the details of how he did it, but it was a most successful business. Sir George Wharton was there, having come to see his son, and he watched our proceedings for some time with great interest. When the place was taken, and it was all over, he called Ernest to him, and said, 'If you take my advice, my boy, you'll be a soldier, and we shall hear something about you by-and-bye.'"

"No, did he?" said Arthur; "and Sir George Wharton too! I'd give something to have him say it of me."

"What did Lord Ernest answer?" inquired Geraldine.

"After his usual fashion, he said nothing; it wouldn't have been Ernest if he had. But Sir George was satisfied, I suppose, for that was the beginning of their acquaintance, and he was a good friend to him for the rest of his life."

"It's a thousand pities his career was cut short," said Arthur, "for every one said he was fit for so much more than the Cape. If there had been a war in Europe, or in India, we should have seen what he really was."

"I certainly am surprised," said Leonie, "at the very high opinion every one has of him, for I should scarcely have thought his talents warranted such entire confidence."

"Oh, you're mistaken there," said Arthur, "that was just his forte. I never knew any one who inspired such thorough confidence. He was not brilliant like some men, but every one felt him to be reliable. We used to say Ernest Fitzgermaine was as good as a brigade in himself, every one had such faith in him."

"But some of his exploits were called dashing," said Geraldine.

"So they were—but he never did a dashing thing for its own sake, though he knew as well as any one that rashness is sometimes prudence. Personally, and as a commander too, I don't think he knew what fear was, but he

was cautious, some people said, to a fault,—
though they were not those best qualified to
judge."

"That is just what I should have said of
him from seeing him go across country," said
Lord Bournemouth. "Often have I watched
Ernest cutting out his work, and followed his
lead too, for even when quite a boy he had
the judgment of fifty, and the pluck of fifteen.
It was beautiful to see him. Well, Arthur,
what do you say to a walk over the turnips
after breakfast? You can have a gun of mine
if you like. I suppose no amount of shooting
will come amiss to you."

"No—you're right there," said Arthur,
"especially if you can lend me a gun, as I
have left mine at Manton's. Cherry-blossom,
we will put off our talk till this evening. If
you don't mind smoke, we'll have it out in my
room towards the small hours."

Geraldine assented, and when her brothers
had gone out, took the papers up-stairs to read
them quietly by herself. What they were we
know already, though no one but herself could
feel all their strong love, all their endurance

through such long hopeless years! We have seen that they had touched even his cold, jealous brother; how must they have seemed to the woman who had the paramount interest in them? True, there was little actually said of her, but that little showed how the thought of her had been the cherished ideal of his heart, how the hope of possessing her at some far distant time had been a spur all through his life, how constantly her image had been with him in all its brightness and purity, a guiding star through many a hard day and weary night! She read them through steadily, no tear fell from her eyes as the brave, hopeful words met them; that record of her dead lover's life-long faith. Rather a solemn gladness filled her; a nobler pride that in this man, great as she now saw him to be, she had inspired so constant an affection. The mists cleared away from his memory, and his character stood out before her, distinct in its grand simplicity, its earnestness, fortitude, indomitable energy, and stedfastness. She did justice not only to his character, but to his in-

tellect, which, developing itself so slowly, had
at last shone out in such clearness; she 'appreciated its strength, its acuteness; she noted
how prompt and vigorous he had been in judgment, how fertile in resource, how energetic in
victory, how undaunted in defeat.

"And I might have been his wife, but for
that one sin!"

It had followed her through life, the consequences of that one almost involuntary sin, but
not a thought of injustice or harshness crossed
her mind; only grateful joy that this crown of
love had not been denied her. Could Ernest
Fitzgermaine have looked down from heaven,
not the deep grief of his companions in arms,
high and low—not a nation's regret and ap-
plause, would have been half as grateful to his
spirit, wearied with waiting and longing for
the whole of his mortal life, as Geraldine's
calm sadness and tearless joy. Unconsciously
his brother had done the best and wisest thing
for him and for her.

"Neither Leonie nor Lindon shall see this,"
she thought. "Of what good would it be?

It shall be my secret till I see *him* once more."

*   *   *   *   *

All through the day she thought of these papers, thought of that time when, as she now discovered, if she had but waited, she would have been his wife, and spared all the horror of her wretched marriage.   And now again the cup was dashed down, just when, unconsciously to herself, it had been held to her lips !   "*Be sure that your sin shall find you out.*"   It had found her out in very truth, and , its consequences pursued her to the last.   This man she could have loved, and her life had been so void of wedded love !   It was not for her, she had forfeited her right to it, had thrown away the chance, and from henceforth she must be given to others, without a thought of herself.   Lindon—Arthur—Leonie, claimed first of all, and should have, all her love, the devotion of all her powers.   Her heart was not buried with Ernest Fitzgermaine, she had too recently discovered what she had lost for that, and she thanked God that it was so, and that she could still give herself up entirely, and almost without regret, to that calm twilight of usefulness and self-denial which was to be her lot..

When evening came she went to Arthur's room, and sat patiently listening while he talked to her of every subject but the one of . which she longed to hear. She forced herself not merely to show, but to feel an interest in all he told her ; he never discovered the slightest difference in her manner while he went on speaking of the Cape, and the people he knew, and the things he had seen there. Now and then, in talking of his regiment, he would mention Lord Ernest, and then Geraldine would try to lead him on, with more or less success.

"Tell me about his death, my dear," she said at length. "You were with him, were you not?"

"From the first moment he was hit; indeed he did not live long after it. I was his aide-de-camp; he was then, you know, temporarily in command of the district, and our regiment was commanded by Major Conyngham, Fitzgermaine looking after it now and then. We always looked forward to those times, for Conyng-

ham was no favourite, and didn't understand
the thing; he was a fidget about trifles, and
was generally in hot water with officers and
men. The Colonel always set things straight,
and every one was sure of justice from him.
I never knew any one more thoroughly impar-
tial and reasonable, and consequently he was
immensely liked, for every one felt he was to
be depended upon."

"Then at this time were you his aide-de-
camp, or still with the regiment?"

"At first I was with the regiment, but he
soon made me his aide-de-camp. You see I
could be useful to him, for I had learnt a good
deal about the Kaffres and their ways, by keep-
ing my eyes about me, and besides, knowing
German, I managed to get on with the Boors;
well—I am making a long story of it, and it
is but a short one really; everything had been
very quiet for some time, so quiet that Fitzgermaine was going to England on some business
of his own, quite thinking the whole thing
settled. Instead of which, we had news one
day that the farm of a Boor, not twenty miles
off, had been attacked, himself and his whole

family murdered, and his cattle driven off.
Soon the whole place was in a blaze—there
were irruptions of savages on all sides, and in
a week the war was going on as actively as
ever. There was no saying how far it might
extend, unless their progress was speedily and
effectually checked. We marched at once to
meet them with what force we could collect,
as it was clear that they meant to give us battle. Their numbers were more than double
ours; however, you know all this, and how
we won, and they were routed and cut to
pieces. If you were a man, I could tell you
exactly how the battle—not that it was more
than a skirmish in civilised warfare, but just
as important as a great battle there—was
fought; but as I don't want to bore you, I'll
go on to the end at once. Stop—that cigar 's
out—hand me the case, Cherry, there 's a dear;
if you will keep me up talking half the night,
I must have another."

Geraldine complied, and Arthur, lighting his
cigar, continued, " It was at the end of the
fight—Fitzgermaine at the head of a handful
of men was pursuing the savages, when one of

them turned round and fired. He was cut
down directly afterwards, but it was too late—
the Colonel was wounded mortally. How
savage our fellows were when they saw him go
down! Some stopped and raised him up
—the greater part continued the pursuit so
fiercely, that on my word I don't believe more
than a couple of hundred or so of the Kaffres
got off. I was among those who stopped, for
I saw directly how it was. He knew it himself, and said, 'It's all up with me, my lads;
carry me back to yonder tree, for I have a
word or two to say before I die.' Four of us
did so, in a blanket which was taken off one
of the dead savages; I walked beside him,
and tried to support him as well as I could.
He must have suffered agonies, but he never
moved a muscle of his face,—only his voice
shook a little. We took him to the tree,
which stood some way apart, and laid him
down in the shade. By this time the
news had spread, and the principal officers
hurried to the spot; the men were already
gathering round, and I never in my life saw
such grief as was on their faces. He called

me, asked if I had a piece of paper and pencil, dictated the despatch you saw in the papers, and then gave his directions as calmly and clearly as ever he had done in his life. About his private affairs he never said a word—I don't think he thought of them once—but towards the end he became very impatient for Conyngham's arrival, for whom he had sent directly. I heard him say, ' Why doesn't he come? It will soon be too late.' At last Conyngham came, and Fitzgermaine motioned to us all to move away, while they talked together for a quarter of an hour or so. Hand me that glass of water, Cherry—this talking makes me thirsty."

"What do you think he said to him?" said Geraldine.

" Oh, I have no doubt he remonstrated with him on his mismanagement of the regiment, and advised him how to do better, for, you see, by his death Conyngham became the Lieutenant-Colonel. I believe myself he had often done so before in private, and stood between us and a good deal of annoyance when we did not suspect it, for he

never publicly reprimanded subordinates in a
responsible position, if it could be avoided.
All we knew was that he talked very earnestly,
and when he had ended, and shook Conyngham's hand, Conyngham turned away, and
we who were near could see that the tears
were rolling down his cheeks. But so they
were down those of many a man not much
used to such things.   When Conyngham had
gone, we gathered round again, for you may
be sure that we did not wish to lose one of
his last words or looks.   He had said everything connected with public business by this
time, and began taking leave of us, saying
a word or two to a good many.   He sent a
message to his regiment generally, which was
given through Conyngham the next morning,
and will not, I think, be soon forgotten.
Well—just then Colonel Montgomerie came
up, who had always been his great friend, and
when he saw him, he looked up with just the
old bright light in his eyes, and on his kind
handsome face—you remember what a good-
looking man he was—and said, 'You are
just in time, Frank, and I am very glad

you are.' Poor Montgomerie knelt down by him, very quietly, but his face looked ten years older in a minute. He tried to speak, but his voice failed, and he bent down and kissed Fitzgermaine's hand, who looked up with a smile, and said, 'Thank you, Frank. Good-bye, and God bless you. Don't forget me. Where is Captain Vivian?'

"I was at his side in a moment, but his eyes were growing dim, and he wandered a little. 'You will see her,' he said, in a whisper; ' and you can tell her—' and there his voice died away. I put my ear down to his mouth, he whispered a word or two that I could not make out—then he shivered, his eyes opened suddenly and very wide, his head fell back, and it was all over."

Arthur stopped short, and as Geraldine stole a look at him, she saw that his eyes were dim with tears — nor could she see very clearly herself. He was silent for several minutes, and then continued, " I can't describe to you how desolate the whole place seemed for the loss of that one man. Every one who knew him, however slightly, felt he

had lost a friend; every one felt that the
head—the one to whom all had looked for
direction and support—was gone. Every man
in the army who could get a bit of crape, put
it on his arm, and I believe many people in
Cape Town wore mourning. There were
great rejoicings among the savages when
they knew that the White Warrior — the
Kaffre's Scourge, as they called him in their
language—was dead; and, in fact, it pretty
nearly undid the effect of our victory. How
it has gone since, I don't know, having been
sent home at once with the despatches, and
with Fitzgermaine's effects. I only know I
have been gazetted to the majority; I wish I
knew who he meant when he said ' You will
see her ;' or whether he really meant anything,
or was only wandering. He did not strike me
as the man for that kind of thing, and yet he
spoke clearly too."

" Most men, whether they seem likely or
not, have an affair of that sort once in their
lives," said Geraldine, quietly. " Thank you,
Arthur, love ; you should tell this to Lindon ;
he would like to hear it."

" No, I don't care to go over it again ; I
tell you anything you ask for, but I should not
have told it to you without. I wish you could
have seen him, Cherry, as I did, when he was
lying in his coffin with his face quite calm,
and a kind of smile on his. lips. But for a
slight contraction of the muscles round the
mouth, you never could have told in what
torments he had died. We all went to look at
him, and I heard many men say that, much as
they had liked his face in life, they never liked
it so well as then, when they saw it. set and
quiet for the last time."

" I dare say," said Geraldine. " I can quite
fancy that."

" Do you remember, Cherry, when you
were in the school-room, and he came and
stayed at Avonbury ? How I enjoyed it, and
the rides we had together, and the fishing
and cricket. It was just like his good-nature,
taking so much notice of such a little chap as
I was. My favourite castle in the air at that
time was that he should marry you—for I
always used to have a fancy that he liked you,
and I should spend the holidays with you."

As he said this, Geraldine's heart smote her —so strangely, in looking back on events which have had large and important consequences, do we sometimes dwell with regret on the most trifling details—as she thought how easily she might have accomplished her brother's childish wish.

" I was never to make a home for you, my dearest," she said sadly — " though had I known—, Arthur, I hear nothing of any one coming to take my place in your heart."

" Oh, a wife, do you mean? No one will ever take your place ; I dare say I shall marry some day, but I shall never find, and never expect to find, your equal. My wife must be second to you, and I shall tell her so. There is only one Cherry-blossom in the world."

" You will prepare a peaceable home for yourself, if you begin with such an understanding," said Geraldine, smiling. " Your wife must be very meek to take it patiently."

" Yes, I have no ambition to marry a splendid creature like Leonie, though I like her with all my heart for a sister-in-law. And she is just the wife for the head of the house. But, for my part, I will have nothing to do with any woman who wants to be my first object."

"Wait till the right woman really comes, and then see what you say," said Geraldine. "Do you hear the church clock striking three? I must not stay longer."

It was mere disinclination to talk made her go, for she never closed her eyes in sleep all that night. She lay thinking of the days that now seemed so far off, and remembered how she had called Lord Ernest dull and heavy, and had not attached any importance to the trifling attentions by which she could now guess he had sought to feel his way. How blind she had been! Worse than blind, for if she had not committed that one fatal fault, her eyes would have been opened, and all the misery of her life been spared her. It had been entirely her own doing, that wreck of her happiness. And he had been so much too good and great for her, and she had so little guessed it.

All through the remainder of the night these thoughts tormented her, and it was not till the morning broke, and the sun burst out

over the beech woods, and streamed into her
room, that the "conclusion of the whole matter" shaped itself clearly in her mind.   The
sin was forgiven, she felt sure, though the
consequences followed her still.   And God is
so good, and so wondrously and mercifully do
the things which seem, and which are, designed as punishments, turn out for our best
happiness and highest advantage in the complicated scheme of this world, that who could
tell if this also might not prove to be the thing
of all others that best fitted herself, and best
promoted the pleasure and good of those
around her, who had deserved more pleasure
than herself? She had some vague perception
on her mind that it might be better for herself
and others that she should be free;—not only
from Leonie's words, for to them she attached
little importance, but because there does seem
at times to be a presentiment granted us of
coming events, either for good or for evil.

CHAPTER VI.

It was a Lusitanian lady, and she was lofty in
    degree—
Was fairer none, nor nobler, in all the realm than
    she.—SPANISH BALLAD.

ARTHUR did not stay very long at Avonbury,
having friends in different parts of England,
whom he was naturally anxious to see before
going back to the Cape, which he was to do
shortly. He promised, before leaving, to return and spend some time with his brother
and sister, and with that promise Geraldine
was fain to be content. She could not object
to his popularity, though she herself was the
greatest sufferer by it, and therefore resigned

herself to only seeing him a fortnight more before he left, consoling herself by thinking that
she would not for the world have him less
fond of his profession.

During his month's absence, Mr Fitzgermaine returned to the Rectory, Lady Anne
having gone to Dorchester to stay with her
father and mother. He brought a sad account
of them;—the blow had been so entirely un-
looked for, they had so entirely persuaded
themselves that nothing could happen to Ernest, that they were completely prostrated.
He had been their pride, and the glory of their
house; from Lord Fitzgermaine they could
derive little satisfaction; especially since, as
soon as possible after his brother's death, he
had gone to the Continent, and by indirect
reports they learnt that he appeared more than
ever fascinated by the beautiful Countess
Luitpolde von Fürstenberg. When Arthur
returned, he said that the fact of their marriage was everywhere believed, though he himself could only ascertain that it was likely to
take place very shortly. Altogether no one
at the Castle was surprised when Mr Fitzger-

maine came one morning and said, " I had a letter from Anne to-day, and they are in great distress at Dorchester. Fitzgermaine is going to marry an Austrian, and my uncle is furious."

" Who is it ? Luitpolde von Fürstenberg ? " inquired Arthur.

" Yes ; do you know anything about her ? " said Mr Fitzgermaine. " I hear she is of a very good family, and they say rich, so I did not understand their objecting to her myself. As to their being hurt at his marrying so soon after Ernest's death, it is only natural ; and I confess I gave Fitzgermaine credit for better taste, if not better feeling."

" What is she like ? Will she be kind to Claribel ? " inquired Geraldine.

" Why, that is what I think the worst part of the business. He writes to say that as Luitpolde is not fond of children, he hopes Anne will keep Claribel, and sends a handsome remittance. I think that looks bad for a beginning."

" So it does," said Leonie ; " but if all I am told of the Countess Luitpolde be true, Claribel is better off with Lady Anne. I have heard about her from several people, for she is well known—rather notorious, in fact, both in London and Paris. She is very handsome, and a great flirt, fast in her tastes and habits, a splendid rider and pistol shot, and much addicted to ' *la chasse*,' both in the English and French sense of the term."

" She was going about in London just before I went to the Cape," said Arthur; " that was five years ago, and she wasn't a chicken then. Very amusing and clever ;—too much so, if anything ; and hard as a nail ;—not the sort of woman one would look to marry."

" I am very sorry to hear all this," said Mr Fitzgermaine, reflectively. " I had hoped Fitzgermaine would have married some nice Englishwoman."

" Ah — perhaps he couldn't get a nice Englishwoman," suggested Lord Bournemouth. " I am glad he has thought of the remittance."

" So am I ;—not that we want it, for Mr Paget provides her with clothes, and everything she can possibly require. But Fitzgermaine ought to do it ; so I am glad he remembered it. I suppose we shall hear of the marriage shortly, if it has not taken place already. Anne says that the only good thing she can see in the business is that it keeps my uncle and aunt from dwelling so exclusively on Ernest's loss. Sometimes two troubles are better than one in that way, and I hope this may prove so. I am glad to see you have lost your cold, Lady Bournemouth."

" Yes, thank you, completely. This fine mild weather suits me, and I hope to be quite strong before we have any fogs or frosts. It is fortunate that I can go out now, if Lady Anne is not coming back."

"At present I am sure it is better for her to be away, and she is more useful there than here ; so I have told her to stay as long as she is wanted. But I must wish you good morning, for I am going to Bristow at once."

"The poor Duke!" said Leonie, when he had gone; " really this is trouble upon trouble. I can scarcely conceive any one more objectionable than the Countess Luitpolde as a daughter-in-law. However, I dare say they won't see much of her. Arthur, did I tell you that I had a letter from Gertrude Kincardine this morning to say that she is coming to England with her husband and children, and proposes to spend a week here ? "

" Before I leave ? "

" Not if you leave in a fortnight. Is it inevitable ? "

" Quite, I am afraid. But I wish I did not miss her. What is she like ? pretty as ever ? "

" Prettier, far," said Geraldine. " She is quite lovely. What must be, must be, I suppose; but it is a pity you can't see her."

" When shall you have a real long furlough, Arthur ? " said Lord Bournemouth. " This counts for nothing."

" No — this is merely accidental," said Arthur. " If the war had been over when we hoped it was, I should have had my furlough then; now I shall have to wait till it is, I dare say. Anyhow it would be a pity to come back while there is anything going on, for one never knows when and where there may be fighting again; and it does not do to miss one's opportunity in the army, any more than in any other profession."

"That's true," said Lord Bournemouth; "still, one can't be always at the height of patriotism and ambition, and this sort of glimpse of you is very tantalizing. However, anything is better than country quarters."

"Anything," said Arthur. "I had enough of that when I first joined. I dare say S—— was a bad specimen; but the dulness, the stupidity, the utterly inane twaddle of the whole thing was detestable."

"I remember your writing that you had made a great mistake, and the army was a gigantic take-in," said Lord Bournemouth. "I forget what you said of your brother officers, but something not precisely civil."

"They deserved it, and a great deal more," said Arthur. "It was much better when we went abroad, but at the time I joined the depôt, the staple of conversation was what Fanny Chalmers said to Brown, whether

Jones's mare could take that fence Graham Burt's horse had refused, and how little Lucy Penny had nearly caught young Robinson. Very interesting to the principals, I dare say, and to most of the by-standers, but, unfortunately, I was not one of them."

"And a very good thing too," said Lord Bournemouth. "Better be dull and bored in such a set than become used to it. What in the world did you do with yourself?"

"I'm |sure I don't know—read every book I could lay my hands on, walked and rode all over the country, and made acquaintance with one or two nice families. Then I and some others were ordered out; at which I was delighted, and every one said, ' Just like that young prig Vivian.'"

"How do you like the idea of going back to it?"

"Oh, well enough—as one likes any road that leads to one's journey's end. I shouldn't mind going somewhere else, provided it was on active service."

"Active service!" said Lord Bournemouth; "well, I am glad I'm not you. But I don't know whether I am any better off as it is. If you go on climbing the ladder at your present rate, there will soon be nothing to choose between your responsibilities and mine, except that the balance will be considerably in my favour; and what a thing that is to think of!"

Arthur smiled gravely.

"I never had your dread of responsibility, Lindon; and shall not shrink from it if it comes. My fear would be staying at the bottom of my profession, not working to the top of it."

"That's right," said Lord Bournemouth, "I see you will get on. No fear of your not being quite near enough to the top, though I don't suppose we shall live to see you replace Ernest."

"Replace him! don't think of it," said Arthur. "If I had his head — which I haven't—I should still want his character. Character goes quite as much to make up success as intellect."

"More, very often," said Leonie; "and that, I suppose, was Lord Ernest's strong point."

"Certainly you and he were as unlike as two men could possibly be, even allowing for the difference of age and position," said Lord Bournemouth. "There was a weight and force about him, which I don't perceive in you. Let us hope you will make it up in some other way."

"Talent apart, I shall never have his prudence and foresight," said Arthur; "my gifts don't lie that way. But all kinds of bricks are good to build something with, I suppose."

"You have become a bit of a philosopher since you have seen the world, Arthur," said Lord Bournemouth. "If you have any more of the like to impart, it had better be done out of doors, for I am going out. You come too, for there are some of the old people here have been asking after Mr Arthur, and we can stroll round the place, and call upon them."

"All right; — I dare say I shan't have another day; and in any case, if a thing of that sort has to be done, it is as well to do it at once."

They went out, and walked for two or three hours, talking meanwhile more intimately than they had done since Arthur's return. Lord Bournemouth was pleased with his brother, and delighted to find him so companionable; and Arthur, after all the eulogies he had received from every quarter, had seldom been so gratified with anything as with Lord Bournemouth's frank confidence and tone of perfect equality.

"You have done an immense deal here," he said, after they had walked through the park and the village; "tell me frankly, Lindon, is it your work, or Leonie's?"

"Quite as much mine as hers, I am thankful to say," was Lord Bournemouth's amused answer. "I see you don't believe in the possibility of my independent action. To tell the truth, it is a struggle from beginning to end, and I wish with all my heart I could conscientiously escape from it. But that is not to be thought of;—I must go on as I have begun, to the end of my life. I am glad you approve; once or twice I have been afraid you might dislike to find alterations; not in the village, of course, but in the house and grounds."

" Oh, no—I like everything you have done, and, without doubt, the place wanted it. It had gone sadly to rack and ruin. I am glad I have seen you all so comfortably settled here. It will be something pleasant to think of when I am out at the Cape. You can't think how I used to worry myself at times about Geraldine. Though I knew she was safe with you, I used to turn it all over in my mind, and wonder if it were possible that Lawrance should recover, and come back to her."

" My dear Arthur! I could have told you he could not. Did not I write explicitly? Why did you not write to me about it? "

" Well—I knew it was nonsense, and that you would have told me if there had been any chance of it. And the fact was, Lindon, I did not know you as well as I do now, and scarcely liked to trouble you with a mere fidget."

" I hope there will be an end of that sort of thing now, Arthur," said Lord Bournemouth, seriously. " Remember all your worries are

mine, as far as you choose to communicate
them; and the more you write, the better I
shall be pleased. If you had written before,
I should have told you that, with my will, Geraldine should never have gone back to
her husband, and that I have been laying by
for her in case of my death. Besides which,
I know Leonie has left her something in her
will. Are you satisfied?"

"Yes, quite; I never had a doubt that you
would do all you could for her; it was only of
her husband, and her own sense of duty, that
I was afraid. Do you think she will ever
marry again?"

"No, I don't; though she might if she
chose, for when we have people staying with
us, I can see that she is just as attractive as
ever, though to a different stamp of men.
But I don't think she has ever seen any one
she really liked; and if she wished to marry
for position, I suppose she would have had
Fitzgermaine."

"What a wife she would have made for
any one worthy of her!" said Arthur.

"Ernest, for instance," said Lord Bourne-mouth. "He would have suited her precisely, and I know he liked her at one time. That was before she ran away, and he had no money to marry upon at that time, so it all died away, and I don't think she ever knew any thing about it."

"Did she not?" said Arthur, absently.

He was thinking of Lord Ernest's last words, and of Geraldine's constrained manner when he commented upon them. Arthur's intense affection for his sister gave him an instinctive perception of her thoughts and feelings, and now, in one moment, the truth flashed upon him. He determined to find out from her exactly how the matter stood, and did so that very evening. Geraldine told him everything, and gave him the papers to read, feeling that there was not a syllable in them that could in any way discredit Lord Ernest, or lower him in her brother's eyes. She made him promise not to say a word about it to Lindon or Leonie, and he did not; it remained to the end of his life another, but a secret bond between him and Geraldine.

He left England at the end of the fortnight ;
Lord Bournemouth and Geraldine going to
Portsmouth to see him embark. Of Leonic
he took leave at Avonbury, as the weather was
too foggy to allow of her travelling. She saw
him alone and said, " Good-bye, dear Arthur ;
I can't tell you how glad I am to have seen
you once more, or how I have enjoyed your
visit. It is so fortunate you were able to come
now, for one never knows how things may turn
out."

" No," said Arthur, thinking she referred
to him. " I may be shot before I get my
furlough."

" I was not thinking of that," said Leonie,
" there is the same uncertainty for us all, and
the Cape is a long way off! There is my
portrait that Lindon promised you—I hope it
won't take up too much room ; it is rather
larger than his and Geraldine's."

" You may be sure I will find room for it,
whatever else I leave behind. Write to me
sometimes when Lindon is busy, and tell me
all about him, and how he is getting on ;—
he will tell me about you and Geraldine."

And so they parted, and often in after years Arthur thought of her words, and wondered why he had not seen their meaning more clearly.

But, for the present, his preparations for departure occupied his attention. Then came the parting from his brother and sister, and then he sailed for the Cape, whence the news that reached them of him, from time to time, amply confirmed Lord Bournemouth's predictions.

They returned to Avonbury and Leonie, to receive Gertrude and Sir Henry, who were now expected in a week or ten days.

CHAPTER VII.

> Stay not thou—
> Man must use haste, for death steals up and up,
> And wins us like a quiet coming tide.
> A heart that God with holy thoughts hath flooded,
> With lustral water for the stainèd world,
> Dares not dole out in niggard drops the wealth,
> Turning full bounty to a scantling dew,
> *That* life must be a torrent.   LENAU.

GERTRUDE's first remark on arriving at
Avonbury was, " Leonie, you look the ghost
of yourself ! "

The emphatic way in which she said it
startled Lord Bournemouth.

"What do you mean? She looks just the same as usual," he said.

"I dare say you think so, because you are with her every day, but I see a great difference," returned Gertrude.

"Henry, is not Leonie altered?"

"You certainly don't look as well as when I saw you last," returned Sir Henry. "If I did not know to the contrary, I should think you had just got over a severe illness."

"Would to Heaven she had got over it!" was Lord Bournemouth's mental exclamation.

"You must not stand discussing my health," said Leonie; "an amusing subject, really! Perhaps you will be good enough to think of something better to talk about. Gertrude, you will find all sorts of improvements here since your time; I must take you all over the place to-morrow."

"That is just what I shall like," said Gertrude; "and I must see your village, and schools, and reading-rooms, and all your plans. I am going to learn a great deal while I am with you; not that it will be of much use to me, but still I like to learn."

There was a great alteration in Gertrude since we last saw her. She was far more plainly dressed, and her manners had become more staid and matronly; partly to be accounted for by the circumstance that a second little boy had been added to her family, to increase her cares and responsibilities. Leonie commented on this fact when they were alone together.

"Yes," said Gertrude, "I really think I am becoming sage. You see it is not respectable for the mother of a family to be always involved in difficulties."

"And how goes the financial department?" said Leonie, smiling.

"*Benissimo!* I have actually repaid Henry fifteen hundred pounds; I have saved some hundreds each year—and really I was quite astonished to find how few dresses I wanted when I began economising. I shall not let Henry continue to give me the full thousand a year when I have paid him; for I find I can dress on five hundred quite well. And he will be glad of it to spend on the cottages. I have begun to see more of the people now; for when Geraldine wrote and told me how much you were doing, I felt quite ashamed of my own idleness. But my people are so different from yours, and live in such a different way, that I am afraid I shall not be able to apply any of your plans. However, I dare say you can give me a good many useful hints."

"I will show you all I can; but, after all, one can only learn by experience."

"To think of my having all my experience to gain at my age! It is shocking, the way in which I have wasted my time. If I had died two years ago, I should not have done a single useful thing since I came into the world, and only abused the money and influence that was intrusted to me," said Gertrude, gravely. "And the torment I have been to poor Henry. And he thinking so differently all the while, that I wonder he did not lose all patience with me."

"You have a great deal to be thankful for; time, and health, and strength, and opportunities for repairing your faults, in the first place," said Leonie, sighing.

"Why do you sigh so sadly?" said Gertrude. "You have not wasted your time and abused your opportunities."

"We have all done those things which we ought not to have done, and left undone those things which we ought to have done," replied Leonie. "If I could begin my life over again, I hope I should act very differently."

"But you have still time, if there is anything you want to amend," said Gertrude, rather startled at her manner.

"Perhaps not; who can tell?" replied Leonie dreamily. But you must tell me some news. Captain Kincardine and his wife have been staying with you, have they not?"

"Oh, yes; and I like them better every day. You know I used to be rather afraid of Willie, because I always felt sure he did not think me good enough for Harry. But this time we got on exceedingly well; and then little Amy comes out wonderfully on acquaintance."

"I always liked her since the night that she fell down and hurt her shoulder," said

Leonie. "How do you think Geraldine is looking?"

"Very well indeed. Oh, do tell me if it is true that Lord Fitzgermaine proposed to her before he married that horrid Austrian?"

"Quite true."

"Was not there something about him during her husband's life-time? Mr Lawrance was jealous of him, or something?"

"I should not tell you if there had been," replied Leonie quietly. "But he proposed to her about ten weeks ago, and she refused him because she did not like him, so there you have it all."

"Well—how any one could like Geraldine, and then marry Luitpolde von Fürstenberg, passes my comprehension," said Gertrude.

"There are more things in heaven and earth than are dreamt of in our philosophy," returned Leonie, laughing; "I dare say pique is not dreamt of in yours."

The next day Gertrude was escorted by Leonie all round the village, and as she affirmed that she had acquired a great deal of useful information, we will hope that such was the case. At all events, if she did not, it was not for want of listening attentively, observing closely, and asking a great many questions. On several succeeding days she also insisted on going to the village, and always returned from these expeditions very thoughtful and silent. Geraldine would have liked to have stopped them, for she felt certain that Leonie was over-exerting herself, but she was so anxious to show, and Gertrude to see, that they would neither of them listen to her remonstrances. The last day was cold and raw, and she tried hard to persuade Leonie to stay at home, and let her go instead; but Leonie laughingly declared that she would allow no coddling, and that with a thick shawl and veil she should catch no cold. But when she returned, she had nearly lost her voice. She came down to dinner, and sat shivering all the evening, though she wore a high velvet gown, and both the dining-room and drawing-room were very warm. Geraldine was seriously uneasy, but Lord Bournemouth did not remark

that anything was amiss, till Sir Henry observed as they were smoking together, " How
wretchedly ill Lady Bournemouth looks."

" Do you think so?" said Lord Bournemouth. " But every one looks wretched when
they have a cold."

" But I thought her very much altered when
I first saw her," persisted Sir Henry.

" Oh, but she had a bad cold on her chest
then."

" Two months before. She ought to have
shaken it off long ago. I don't wish to alarm
you, Bournemouth; but West Indian consti-
tutions are uncertain things."

Lord Bournemouth looked very much disturbed.

" What would you advise me to do? What
would you do in my place?"

" If she were my wife, I would take her up
to London, and have the best advice for her.
A winter in some warm climate might do her
a great deal of good."

" I will take her as soon as she is
well enough to go!" exclaimed Lord

Bournemouth. "To-morrow if her cold is better."

He left the room, and ran up-stairs to Leonie, who was lying in bed, under a quantity of blankets and quilts, and supported by a large pile of pillows. "Are you worse, Leonie?" he asked.

"Rather. I am going to have a very bad cold on my chest, I think. I can scarcely breathe."

"I shall take you to London when you are better, to consult Spence Wilson, and see if he doesn't think you had better go abroad for the winter. Should you not like to go to the West Indies again?"

"Should I not? Oh, Lindon, how delightful it would be! And the sea voyage!"

"When shall you be able to go to London?"

"I don't know; the sooner the better, for if I wait till my cold is really bad, it may be weeks before I can move."

"Could you go to-morrow?"

"Perhaps, if the day is fine. You must get

Geraldine to come with me, if she does not mind it."

And as the next day proved warm and clear Leonie was dressed in an infinity of wraps, carefully packed up in an invalid carriage, and departed for London with her husband and Geraldine. She bore the journey better than they had expected, and saw Dr Spence Wilson the next day. He spoke hopefully, as was that eminent physician's' usual habit, sounded her lungs, and said that there was no positive disease. He decidedly forbade her remaining in England for the winter, and on hearing that the West Indies was her native country, and that she had a great wish to return there, said that it would be the best place for her; but that she must not think of starting till this cold had gone.

Geraldine went to him after he had left Leonie, and said, " I am afraid you think more seriously of my sister-in-law's case than you say? Is there any immediate danger?"

"None—none, I assure you. I am convinced that her lungs are sound at present.

There is congestion, but no disease. You must take great care of her. This cold is a most unfortunate thing, just as she ought to be leaving England."

" Will she ever be able to live in England?"

" That I can't tell; she says that hitherto it has not disagreed with her. But it will be necessary, I think, to go abroad for the winter, for some years, at all events."

" And you are sure her lungs are sound?"

" Perfectly; but, to tell you the whole truth, if once they were affected, there would be very little to hope. Cases of consumption are generally very rapid among West Indians, and her constitution is very far from strong. Everything depends on how she gets over this cold. When she is once fairly off, there will be comparatively little danger."

" And if her lungs should become affected, you will tell me and her? You need not be afraid—she is ready to die, and it will neither agitate nor excite her."

" As far as that can be said of any one, it may of her, I know," replied Dr Wilson.

"Lord Bournemouth was much the most agitated. Well—I will certainly tell her, though I sincerely hope there will be no need. But it is not certain that the case would terminate fatally, even then ; I have known some remarkable cures effected in the West Indies."

The cold went on from bad to worse, but not worse than Leonie had had them lately. Dr Wilson came every day; once or twice he brought another doctor of eminence to consult with him, but they were both certain that nothing was seriously wrong with the lungs.

One day Gertrude, who was in London with her husband, came to see her. They talked together for some time, very quietly, for quiet was imperatively ordered ; so Gertrude subdued her voice to a whisper, and carefully chose unexciting topics. But when she left Leonie's room, she went to the one where Geraldine was sitting, ran up to her, and falling on her knees, buried her face in her lap, saying in a voice choked with sobs, " Oh, Geraldine, she is dying! I know she is !"

" No, she is not, Gertrude," replied Geraldine; "my dear child, you must not alarm yourself in this way ; humanly speaking, the chances are all in favour of her recovery."

"Oh no, no ; I never saw any one such a colour, and she is a perfect skeleton, and she talks as if she were going to die !"

"I believe," said Geraldine, forcing herself to speak calmly, "that for some time Leonie has fancied that she was likely to die young. But as she could not say she had the symptoms of any particular disease she never consulted any one, though it would have been far better if she had, for it appears that though she has always been perfectly well, her constitution is excessively delicate, with a decided tendency to consumption. But she never felt ill, and it was more a kind of presentiment than anything else. The first thing that alarmed us was these severe colds on her chest, which she never had till this autumn."

"Oh, but presentiments are always true !"

"That is superstitious, Gertrude. Don't you think it very likely that Leonie, feeling weak and unwell, without being able to assign any particular cause for it, should think it was not improbable that, if she were attacked by any definite illness, she would not have strength to get over it?"

"But what do you think yourself?"

"When first I came up to London I was exceedingly alarmed ; but both doctors have assured me that her lungs are perfectly sound, and that a winter in the West Indies will probably set her up again. So I hope that, with care, she may get over this crisis ; for crisis it is, I feel convinced."

"And she so young!" sighed Gertrude, rather reässured, however. "Oh, Geraldine, I do love her so! She helped me and advised me in all those miserable difficulties ; she made me think seriously, she stopped me when I was losing Henry's esteem by my follies! If I am worth anything now, it is all her doing. And she is so good, and so grand!"

Poor Gertrude again sunk her head on Geraldine's lap, and burst into tears, in which Geraldine was forced to join; her assumed fortitude having completely broken down.

"This is very wrong," she said, at length. "I ought to go to her; she must not be left alone. Come, Gertrude, cheer up; God is merciful, and her fate is in His hands."

"I will go home and pray for her," whispered Gertrude.

"And 'the prayer of faith shall save the sick,'" returned Geraldine. "Come, let me put on your shawl."

Gertrude departed, and Geraldine went back to Leonie.

"How long you have been away!" said she. "Has Gertrude only just left?"

"That is her carriage going now."

"Oh, then I am glad you did not hurry yourself. I am getting dreadfully selfish! Of course you had a great many things to talk about, but I shan't ask what they were, for I am going to be perfectly quiet all the rest of the evening. Do you know that my cold is much better to-night?"

"No, is it really? I am so glad! Then we shall be off soon?"

"I hope so. It is very good of you to

come with me. I hope you don't mind
leaving England? "

"I like it of all things. To winter abroad
has always been one of my favourite dreams,
and now that it comes coupled with a duty, it
is positively delightful."

"So delightful that I don't dare think of
it, for fear it should never come to pass. Not
that that would be a loss to me, but I should
be so sorry for you and Lindon, for I think
you would miss me."

"You know I should," was all Geraldine
could trust herself to answer.

But Leonie really seemed better; so she
forced herself to look on the bright side of
things, and hope for the best, though she
tried to moderate Lord Bournemouth's sanguine expectations of starting by the beginning of next week. However, Geraldine herself did not think it improbable when she
got up next morning, and found that Leonie
had had a good night, quiet and comfortable, though she had not slept much. The
oppression on her chest was gone, and she

began to talk hopefully of starting in a few
days.   She asked Geraldine to bring her her
writing things, and help her to remember
all the various directions she wished to give
to Lady Anne about the parish.   There
was a good deal to think of and arrange,
so much that Geraldine begged her to
postpone part of it till the next day; but she
could not bear putting it off, and went on
till she was thoroughly tired out.

" There are a few more things that I must
tell you about, in case I die; for my mind
will not be at rest till my affairs are settled.
My will is in the pocket of my writing-case;
of course it is not a legal one; but I am sure
Lindon will attend to all my wishes.   I have
left you an annuity.   And I have left a legacy
to my maid, and you must send her back
to her friends in the West Indies, and pay
her passage.   Then there are one or two
sums for charities to which I have been
in the habit of subscribing.   As to my
jewels, Lindon will have those, except a few
things which I have left as keepsakes.   This

ring," pointing with a smile to a diamond one on her finger, "is for Gertrude. She will know why."

"Leonie," said Geraldine, anxiously, "tell me the exact truth. Do you feel better or worse?"

"Better, decidedly. But I don't feel at all certain of getting over this illness, and I wish to be prepared in all ways. However, I have done enough for to-day, for I am quite tired, and so, I dare say, are you. What a comfort you are to me! If I die, you will live with Lindon and take care of him; so that will be off my mind."

Geraldine longed to beg her not to talk in this way, but she knew that the feeling was wrong, as a Christian's death should be no subject of sadness or regret; so she sat with the tears fast dropping from her eyes, and a sore feeling at her heart.

"Is that all?" she asked.

"Yes, all; so now I will lie down, and we will have a chat about my own country. I must tell you what you will see, and where we shall go, and all about it."

Geraldine was glad to hear her change the subject, though she reproached herself for it, and after settling her comfortably on the sofa, lighted the candle lamp, and sat down to work and talk. In about half an hour, Leonie dropped off into a doze. She had turned round to Geraldine that her head might rest more easily and the soft light of the lamp fell full on her face. What a beautiful, noble face it was, with its sweet, earnest look of calm patience and endurance! Much as Geraldine had always admired her, she had never been so fascinated by this wonderful beauty of expression as now. Lord Bournemouth entered, and went softly up to the sofa. He, too, seemed struck by the same thing, for after standing beside her a few moments, he turned away and whispered, " How good and dear she looks! Geraldine, pray that she may be spared to me!"

" I do, indeed I do, all day long," said Geraldine. " I trust our prayers will be heard. She seems really better to-day."

Lord Bournemouth made no answer. He
had been very much disturbed lately by the
unusual gentleness and affection of Leonie's
manner. It was so unlike her! There came
back to his mind something he had once
chanced to read ; some simile of Coleridge's
concerning the holly, whose young leaves are
sharp and prickly when it has to defend itself
against all attacks, but which casts off its
weapons as the leaves grow older and stronger
and the battle is won. Was the victory gained, and Leonie laying aside her arms ?

She awoke as he stood by her.

" Back so soon ! " she said.

" Why, it is past seven."

" Is it ? I thought it was only five. I must
have slept longer than I thought. But I am
much better for it. You may soon take our
berths ;—we shall really be off next week,
please God. I have been telling Geraldine all
about the beautiful places she is to see. But
it is my belief she looks forward more to seeing the slaves than anything else."

" I certainly am curious to see them," said

Geraldine. " I want to see how the whole thing looks, and whether the Quadroons and Creoles are as fine a race as people say."

" They are very fine-looking people, a good many of them, and some really handsome. And a thorough-bred, full-blooded negro is by no means to be despised, morally or physically."

" So they tell me, but I confess to a prejudice against them," returned Geraldine.

" Why?—you are quite wrong, depend upon it. I myself have black blood in my veins, and am proud of it."

" Oh, you are joking ! " said Geraldine. " Lindon, is she not ? "

" She is in very sober earnest," he replied. "I told you at first that she was descended from every race that ever was heard of."

" But you haven't a trace of negro blood; and you were born free, were you not ? "

Leonie laughed. " I did not say that either my father or mother was a negro, or my grand-parents either. It was more than a hundred and fifty years ago that my ancestor,

Don Miguel de Medina, settled in Cuba, and married a Quadroon. He never owned to it till the day of his death, though he was really married, as every one knows who knows the story. Like all who have black blood in their veins, we have never entirely lost the traces of our descent, which come out now and then. I, for instance, am strikingly like a portrait of Ines de Medina which we have at home."

"Of course he freed her; but after his death, was there no fear of her being kidnapped, and sold again?"

"Apparently she thought so, for she went to Spain with her son, whom she married to the daughter of an English merchant settled in Seville. His son was like his mother, so like that there was no fear of the negro origin being detected. He returned to Cuba, bought large estates there, and there my family have been ever since."

"And did the estates continue in the family? Did you inherit them and have slaves?"

"I had slaves, but I did not inherit them.

The estates were dissipated long before my father's time, and what money he had was made in trade. He was a merchant. But my first husband, Don Felippo de Sosada, had large estates which he left to me."

"And what did you do with them? Did you try to educate your people? did you free them?" said Geraldine eagerly.

"Like the Lady in Longfellow's Poems? No, I did not; if I had, Lindon would not be quite so well off as he is. Remember I was only seventeen then, and a Spaniard by birth and association. I don't know what I might have done as I grew older and my ideas expanded; but then, you see, Lindon came and married me. I did try to educate them, and involved myself in a good many troubles, and spent a large sum in fines. Then my father, who managed my property for me till I was of age, was displeased, and forbade my doing so any more, and altogether I had a very difficult part to play, and was only too glad to marry an Englishman, and so cut the knot at once."

" Then were they sold? "

" Yes,—I disposed of the whole thing. I would not continue to hold the estates if I could not live on them, and as Lindon's position would not allow of his staying there, my duty coincided exactly with my inclinations, and happy was I when I sailed for England."

Leonie stopped, and looked at her husband. They were both thinking of the time when he had brought her to England, a bright, healthy girl, so full of life and spirit that no one looking at her could have prophesied anything but a long and happy life. He, at least, was now sanguine that she might yet be spared for many years. She appeared so much stronger and more lively, and the cold was evidently so much better, that it seemed not unreasonable to hope that, when once started, all might yet be well.

CHAPTER VIII.

God breathed into this house of clay
The spirit that hath pass'd away,—
Christ gave the true courageous mind,
The noble heart ye no more find.
N. HERMANN, 1560.

She hath escaped all danger now,
  Her pain and sighing all are fled;
The crown of joy is on her brow,
  Eternal glories o'er her shed;
In golden robes, a queen, a bride,
She standeth at her Sovereign's side.
ALLENDORF, 1725.

Ah, broken is the golden bowl, the spirit fled for ever,
Let the bell toll, a saintly soul floats down the Stygian
    river.
And Guy de Vere, hast thou no tear ?   Weep now or
    never more—
See, on yon low and lonely bier, there lies thy love,
    Lenore.   EDGAR POE.

AND the next day, and the next, the improvement continued, slowly but steadily, till
at the end of the week Lord Bournemouth
went to take the berths. The first packet
that started was small, and he was not satisfied with the arrangements ; the cabins were
very close, and if she should have a relapse
on board, it would be important that she
should be as comfortable as possible. But
ten days later a large new packet, the Massachusetts, was to start on her second voyage,
and her accommodation was so very superior
that Dr Wilson agreed with Lord Bournemouth in thinking it far better to wait and go
in her, than incur certain discomfort, and perhaps some risk, by going in one of the smaller
ones. Leonie was pleased with the arrangement, as she hoped, before they left, to be

well enough to go out, and get some things
she wanted for herself. Geraldine, however,
persuaded her to entrust her commissions to
her; with the exception of some books and
drawing materials as a provision for the
voyage. These she insisted on choosing in
person; she delighted in a colour-shop, and
in books was confident that no one could get
what she wanted for her, and that she was
strong enough to go for them herself. With
some difficulty Geraldine persuaded her to
send for the drawing materials, and only attempt the bookseller's. So one sunny morning they drove together to the bookseller's,
and Leonie eagerly began examining the
shelves, and selecting the works she required.
She had miscalculated her strength, as it soon
appeared; before a quarter of an hour had
passed, she began to feel tired, but would say
nothing about it, thinking she should still be
able to finish what she was about without
doing herself any injury. Another half hour
told still more heavily upon her, her weariness
and faintness could be concealed no longer,

and Geraldine, alarmed at her white face, hurried her to the carriage. "How dreadfully tired you look!" she said. "We ought not to have done this—a short drive would have been enough for you."

"I am no more tired than I have a good right to be. But has not the wind got up since we came out? It is so chilly."

"The shop was very close," said Geraldine. "You ought to have taken off your large cloak when you were there. But I guessed how it would be, when we came out; so I brought an extra shawl, and here it is."

"You think of everything," returned Leonie. She was stopped by a fit of coughing, and Geraldine hastened to put the shawl round her, and shut the window. At the door of the hotel they met Dr Wilson.

"How very imprudent!" he said, as he helped her out of the carriage. "The east wind is biting across the Park! I wish I had come two hours ago, as I thought of doing."

" We have not been in the Park—we have been shopping," said Geraldine.

" Worse and worse," he replied; " Lady Geraldine, the fatigue alone is enough to kill her!   You should not have allowed it."

He spoke more sharply than was his wont, for he was greatly alarmed and very much vexed.

" Indeed I could not help it," remonstrated poor Geraldine.   " I did what I could."

Leonie was holding her handkerchief up to her mouth, and would not speak till she was in her own room, and out of the cold air.

" You must not scold her," she then said with a smile.   " It was my doing;—you don't know how self-willed I am."

" Indeed, I suspect so," he said.   " I hope no harm may come of it, but you have done a most foolish thing."

" That I am beginning to be aware of," said Leonie, unfastening her cloak and shawl; " my throat is so uncomfortable,—and I don't like this tight feeling in my chest and pain in my side coming back."

She was deadly pale, with a bright pink spot on each cheek, and her breath came and went quickly.

"It is a little return of cold," said Dr Wilson quietly; "what else can you expect? You will get off better than you deserve if you are able to start in the Massachusetts."

"Oh, you don't say so!" said Leonie; "Lord Bournemouth will be so vexed; he has set his heart on going by her. What shall I do? I will do anything you tell me."

"Too late," was his mental comment, but he replied cheerfully, "That's right; after all, it may be a mere trifle. Now pray lie down; I will arrange your pillows so that you can breathe just as well as if you were standing."

He settled her on the sofa, ordered several remedies to ease her chest, and did not leave her till he had seen them applied.

"It is all very well," he thought, as he got

into his brougham and drove away. "I will do all I can for her, but if I am not much mistaken, this day's work has killed her. Poor thing, it is a sad case, so young and so happy and useful!"

Lord Bournemouth was very much startled and distressed to find his wife so much worse when he came in, and great was his consternation and dismay when he heard what she had been about.

"I hope losing our passage in the Massachusetts may be the worst of it," was all he said.

"Indeed I am very sorry," said Leonie, humbly. "It was very wrong of me. How could I be so selfish! Dear Lindon, please don't be angry with me."

"Angry! I'm not angry, my dear one; only very much grieved. You are trifling recklessly with your life."

Leonie's reply was a pleading look, as she took his hand and gently kissed it. Again Lord Bournemouth was startled. Only once before had she ever kissed him unasked, and that was when he had told her that her having on children was not a subject of grief to him, as she had feared.

" Do you want to make up, and be friends, you naughty child ? " he said.

" Yes, 1 do—I don't want to have the shade of a difference," she replied, gravely and em- phatically.

" Then do what I order, and that is not to speak a word more till I give you leave."

But he might take what care of her he liked ;—the mischief was done. It was many days before he would own the fact, though she grew visibly worse every hour, with very few fluctuations. She suffered a great deal, espe- cially from pain in her side ; sometimes she could scarcely bear it. She did bear it, how- ever, bravely and patiently, with calm trust and submission. There was no longer any talk of going by the Massachusetts, for Leonie was in bed, and had been so for a week when she started. Then again she rallied, and, though confined to her room, was able to get up and lie on the sofa for the greater part of

the day.   But a bitter east wind set in, and
notwithstanding that every precaution was
taken, she felt its effects, and it aggravated her
cough fearfully.   Dr Wilson was sent for down
into the country to attend a patient who was
supposed to be dying.   He was absent for
four days, and during that time Leonie would
not see any one else, saying that she should do
very well till he came back.   He came to see
her as soon as he returned.

"I hope I don't find you worse?" he said,
on entering.

"Better, in one sense," she replied, "for I
don't think I have much longer to live.   Have
you brought your stethoscope?"

"Yes, certainly;—but I hope this is only
your own fancy."

"I have been spitting blood constantly since
you left," she replied quietly.   "But I said
nothing to my husband or sister about it,
thinking it better to wait till I heard your
opinion."

He made no answer, but produced his
stethoscope, and busied himself about apply-

ing it.   He kept his ear at the orifice for a long time before he seemed satisfied.

"Well," she said, smiling, "I don't think you need listen so long; it is pretty clear, is it not?   Come—we have agreed that I am to know the truth at once; my lungs are affected, are they not?"

"Both;—the right one is nearly gone;—I have seldom seen so rapid a case.   My dear Lady Bournemouth, I am very sorry."

"Not for me—for my husband and sister. For the last six months I have never expected to see new year's day.   But I should like to die at Avonbury; do you think I could go there in time?"

"You could, certainly, I should think; but, for Lord Bournemouth's sake, I should advise you not to try it.   The journey would be almost certain to hasten your death, and he would never forgive himself.   I know him; he would always think that something else might have been done, or that if you had stayed in London you might have recovered."

"That is true; I see you do indeed know

him. I will give it up. But now you must promise me to let me tell him this myself."

"I am afraid of the effect it will have on you. It will be a terrible shock to him, for I see that he does not realize your danger; and I need not say that agitation is the worst possible thing for you."

"I think he will bear it as well as I know I shall."

"Men have not always the fortitude of women on these occasions. Besides, it is a very different thing for you to die and go to heaven, and for him to be left alone on earth."

Leonie smiled at the Doctor's bluntness.

"You need not be afraid," she said; "I shall know very well how to keep myself calm, and him too."

"You can do anything with him, I know, but this is a very different trial from any to which he has been yet exposed. But I have done; if you really wish it, you shall have your own way. I think I can trust you."

He got up, and shook hands with her warmly. "I shall come again to-morrow."

" *Au revoir*, then ; or no, I will say good-
bye, in case I never see you again. And thank
you very much.   Will you send Lord Bournemouth to me ? "

Lord Bournemouth came in, and was surprised to find her looking so well, for her
conversation with the Doctor had flushed her
cheeks, and made her eyes look bright and
lively.   So, with his usual sanguine nature, he
began to hope.

"You look uncommonly well to-day, Leonie," he said, "and handsomer than ever, for
you have more colour than you used to have.
Don't you feel better ? "

Poor Leonie ! she had not expected this,
and it made her task doubly hard.   She pray-
ed silently for strength and judgment, and then
said, " No, not better.   You know this sort of
consumptive flush is the worst possible sign."

" Oh, you must not take such a gloomy view
of yourself.   Gertrude is here ; won't you see
her ? "

" Lindon," said Leonie, earnestly, " I can't
bear to hear you talk of death as a gloomy

thing. You would not think so if you were going to die yourself, I hope?"

"I hope not," he said, "but that is different."

"Not if it is God's will that I should die. Lindon, dearly as I love you, I can only think of it as a mercy. You will soon follow me; we shall not be separated long; we shall be at Home together."

"Leonie, what do you mean?" he said, now thoroughly alarmed. "Are you really worse? Has Dr Wilson said so? What did he say?"

"You must not overwhelm me with questions," said Leonie, smiling, and stroking his hand. "Yes, my dear, he does not think that I shall live long."

"What did he say? Tell me exactly what he said."

"Gently, gently. He said that both my lungs were affected, and the right one nearly gone."

Lord Bournemouth sat down beside her, buried his face in his hands, and cried like a child. Leonie, greatly as she loved him, much as she disliked to give him pain, was neither

disturbed nor distressed. She knew that she
could comfort him, and waited quietly and intently for the moment of doing so. At last he
looked up.

"And how long does he think you have to
live?"

"Oh dear!" said Leonie in surprise, "I
never thought of asking him. But not long,
I am sure. Dear Lindon, you must not be so
grieved. Perhaps we shall not be separated
long—who can tell? And we are all dying
every day of our lives; it is only one going a
little sooner and one a little later. I have finished my work;—your Father and mine calls
me; your Brother and mine will send the
Comforter to you."

The words might sound common-place; the
manner of saying them was not. She looked
so earnest; it was all so real and present to
her, so completely a part of her daily life, the
thing by which she lived and moved and had
her being. To him, too, it was real and true;
thank God that he could now say so! and he
presently became calm, and listened silently to

her as she gave him some directions about the poor people at Avonbury.

"And you will go on with it all? You will not be disheartened, though it may seem dreary at first?"

"I will, so help me God!"

"You will have Geraldine. She has promised to live with you. I don't think I have anything more to tell you, for I have written down most of my directions. God bless you, my own dear Lindon; I have never been so happy in my life as with you; I thank Him for giving us to one another."

Her voice was lost in the quick, short, panting breath; Lord Bournemouth walked to the window, burying his face in his hands. She got up slowly, and with pain and difficulty crossed the room; though he neither saw nor heard her till she put her arms round his neck, and laying her head on his shoulder, nestled her face against his with a soft, long kiss.

"Leonie! you ought not; let me take you back."

" No, no," she murmured, " it is nearly over
—it is best so, O my Father."

She nestled still closer, and clung to him;
then her weight felt heavier on his arm.
What is this? Why does it grow heavier still?
and is she not colder?

He looked down—raised her head a little—
touched her lips — Oh God! Leonie was
dead.

    *   *   *   *

He lifted up the beautiful dead body, carried
it to the sofa, laid it down very carefully,
smoothed the limbs, closed the eyes, and then,
with one of her hands in his, sat down beside it.
And all this time, not a tear.　There he sat,
very quiet, with no sorrow in his heart—the
time for that had not yet come; it seemed to
him that his soul was still with hers; as if he
had followed her to Paradise.　There he sat
for an hour, though it might have been days
or years, or minutes for all he knew, and then
a knock was heard at the door, and Geraldine's
voice said, " May I come in? Leonie, will you
see Gertrude ? "

Then she came in, softly, for she thought Leonie was asleep.

" Is that you, Geraldine?" said Lord Bournemouth; " you need not be afraid; come in."

She came in, still softly; then, astonished at his look, went quickly up to the sofa. '

" Oh, what is this! Oh, why did you not call me? And she has never said good-bye to me !"

And Geraldine fell on her knees, sobbing.

*   *   *   *

They took their dead down to Avonbury, and buried her there among the people who loved her well, and who came from far and near to her funeral. The choir she had taken such pains to teach, sung

> An anthem for the queenliest dead that ever died
> so young,
> A dirge for her, the doubly dead, in that she died so
> young;

and sung it right nobly, as was fit, though the voice which had been used to lead them was hushed for ever.

And so she rests under the green sod, with

the free winds blowing round her, and the flowers growing above her head. And her memory is still green in the hearts of her husband and sister, who live together, and talk of her often, and think of all she did, and keep up her old customs, and plan new ones, such as would have pleased her well. And now our story is ended, for we have passed the crisis of Geraldine's life, and her stormy days are over, and the remaining ones are spent in calm, sweet piety and usefulness. Lord Bournemouth never married again, and seldom moved from Avonbury, for the last year had aged him much, and his one thought and wish was to rejoin Leonie in heaven. Once he went to the West Indies, and took Geraldine with him, and showed her where he had wooed and won his beautiful foreign bride, and then they returned to where she had lived and worked, and wished to die.

THE END.

JOHN CHILDS AND SON, PRINTERS.

NEW AND INTERESTING WORKS

PUBLISHED BY

MESSRS. HURST AND BLACKETT,

SUCCESSORS TO MR. COLBURN.

MEMOIRS OF THE COURT OF GEORGE IV. FROM

ORIGINAL FAMILY DOCUMENTS. By the DUKE OF BUCKINGHAM AND CHANDOS, K.G. 2 vols. 8vo. with Portraits. 30s. bound.

Among the many interesting subjects elucidated in this work will be found : The Trial of Queen Caroline—The King's Visits to Ireland, Scotland, and Hanover—Female Influence at Court—The Death of Lord Castlereagh—Junction of the Grenville Party with the Government—The Political and Literary Career of George Canning—O'Connell and the Catholic Claims—The Marquess Wellesley in Ireland—The Duke of Wellington's Administration—George the Fourth as a Patron of Art and Literature, &c.

"The country is very much indebted to the Duke of Buckingham for the publication of these volumes—to our thinking the most valuable of the contributions to recent history which he has yet compiled from his family papers Besides the King, the Duke of Buckingham's canvass is full of the leading men of the day—Castlereagh, Liverpool, Canning, Wellington, Peel, and their compeers. We are sure that no reader, whether he seeks for gossip, or for more sterling information, will be disappointed by the book. There are several most characteristic letters of the Duke of Wellington."—*John Bull.*

"These volumes are the most popular of the series of Buckingham papers, not only from the nature of the matter, but from 'the closeness of the period to our own times."—*Spectator.*

"There is much in these volumes which deserves the perusal of all who desire an intimate acquaintance with the history of the period. The comments of well-informed men, like Lord Grenville, and Mr. T. Grenville, disclosing as they do the motives of individuals, the secret movements of parties, and the causes of public events, are of high value to the student, and exceedingly interesting to the general reader."—*Daily News.*

"These volumes are of great intrinsic and historical value. They give us a definite acquaintance with the actions, a valuable insight into the characters, of a succession of illustrious statesmen."—*Critic.*

"The original documents published in these volumes—penned by public men, who were themselves active participators in the events and scenes described—throw a great deal of very curious and very valuable light upon this period of our history. The private letters of such men as Lord Grenville, Mr. T. Grenville, Mr. Charles Wynn, Mr. Freemantle, Dr. Phillimore, and Mr. Plumer Ward, written in the absence of all restraint, necessarily possess a high interest even for the lightest and most careless reader ; whilst, in an historical sense, as an authentic source from which future historians will be enabled to form their estimate of the characters of the leading men who flourished in the reign of the last George, they must be regarded as possessing an almost inestimable value. The more reserved communications, too, of such men as Lord Liverpool, the Duke of Wellington, the Marquis of Wellesley, Sir Henry Parnell, &c., will be received with great interest and thankfulness by every historiographer, whilst the lighter *billets* of Sir Walter Scott and Mr. Henry Wynn will be welcome to every body. Taking this publication altogether, we must give the Duke of Buckingham great credit for the manner in which he has prepared and executed it, and at the same time return him our hearty thanks for the interesting and valuable information which he has unfolded to us from his family archives."—*Observer.*

MEMOIRS OF THE COURT OF THE REGENCY.

FROM ORIGINAL FAMILY DOCUMENTS.   By the DUKE OF BUCKING
HAM AND CHANDOS, K.G.   2 vols. 8vo., with Portraits, 30s. bound.

"Here are two more goodly volumes on the English Court; volumes full of new sayings, pictures, anecdotes, and scenes.   The Duke of Buckingham travels over nine years of English history.   But what years those were, from 1811 to 1820!   What events at home and abroad they bore to the great bourne!—from the accession of the Regent to power to the death of George III.—including the fall of Perceval; the invasion of Russia, and the war in Spain; the battles of Salamanca and Borodino; the fire of Moscow; the retreat of Napoleon; the conquest of Spain; the surrender of Napoleon; the return from Elba; the Congress of Vienna; the Hundred Days; the crowning carnage of Waterloo; the exile to St. Helena; the return of the Bourbons; the settlement of Europe; the public scandals a the English Court; the popular discontent, and the massacre of Peterloo!   On many parts of this story the documents published by the Duke of Buckingham cast new jets of light, clearing up much secret history.   Old stories are confirmed—new traits of character are brought out.   In short, many new and pleasant additions are made to our knowledge of those times."—*Athenæum*.

"Invaluable, as showing the true light in which many of the stirring events of the Regency are to be viewed.   The lovers of Court gossip will also find not a little for their dification and amusement."—*Literary Gazette*.

"These volumes cover a complete epoch, the period of the Regency—a period of large and stirring English history.   To the Duke of Buckingham, who thus, out of his family archives, places within our reach authentic and exceedingly minute pictures of the governors of England, we owe grateful acknowledgements.   His papers abound in fresh lights on old topics, and in new illustrations and anecdotes.   The intrinsic value of the letters is enhanced by the judicious setting of the explanatory comment that accompanies them, which is put together with much care and honesty."—*Examiner*.

MEMOIRS OF THE COURT AND CABINETS OF

GEORGE THE THIRD, FROM ORIGINAL FAMILY DOCUMENTS.   By the DUKE OF BUCKINGHAM AND CHANDOS, K.G., &c.   THE THIRD AND FOURTH VOLUMES, comprising the period from 1800 to 1810 and completing this important work.   8vo., with Portraits.   30s. bound.

"The present volumes exhibit the same features as the former portion of the series The general reader is entertained, and the reader for historical purposes is enlightened. Of their value and importance, there cannot be two opinions."—*Athenæum*.

"These volumes comprehend a period the most important in the events relating to our domestic affairs and foreign relations to be found in the British annals; told, not only by eye-witnesses, but by the very men who put them in motion.   The volumes now published immeasurably exceed their predecessors in interest and importance.   They must find a place the library of every English gentleman."—*Standard*.

HISTORY OF THE REIGN OF HENRY IV., KING OF

FRANCE AND NAVARRE.   From numerous Original Sources.   By MISS FREER.   Author of "The Lives of Marguerite d'Angoulême, Elizabeth de Valois, Henry III," &c.   2 vols. with Portraits, 21s.

LECTURES ON ART, LITERATURE, AND SOCIAL

SCIENCE.   By HIS EMINENCE CARDINAL WISEMAN.   1 vol. with Portrait.   (*In Preparation.*)

HENRY III. KING OF FRANCE AND POLAND;

HIS COURT AND TIMES. From numerous unpublished sources, in·
cluding MS. Documents in the Bibliothèque Impériale, and the Archives
of France and Italy. By MISS FREER, Author of " Marguerite d'Angoulême," " Elizabeth de Valois, and the Court of Philip II," &c. 3 vols.
post 8vo. with fine portraits, 31s. 6d. bound.

"Miss Freer having won for herself the reputation of a most painstaking and trust-
worthy historian not less than an accomplished writer, by her previous memoirs of
sovereigns of the houses of Valois and Navarre, will not fail to meet with a most
cordial and hearty welcome for her present admirable history of Henry III., the last of
the French kings of the house of Valois. We refer our readers to the volumes themselves for the interesting details of the life and reign of Henry III., his residence in
Poland, his marriage with Louise de Lorraine, his cruelties, his hypocrisies, his penances,
his assassination by the hands of the monk Jaques Clément, &c. Upon these points, as
well as with reference to other persons who occupied a prominent position during this
period, abundant information is afforded by Miss Freer; and the public will feel with us
that a deep debt of gratitude is due to that lady for the faithful and admirable manner in
which she has pourtrayed the Court and Times of Henry the Third."—*Chronicle.*

"The previous historical labours of Miss Freer were so successful as to afford a rich
promise in the present undertaking, the performance of which, it is not too much to say,
exceeds expectation, and testifies to her being not only the most accomplished, but the
most accurate of modern female historians. The Life of Henry III. of France is a
contribution to literature which will have a reputation as imperishable as its present
fame must be large and increasing. Indeed, the book is of such a truly fascinating
character, that once begun it is impossible to leave it."—*Messenger.*

"Among the class of chronicle histories, Miss Freer's Henry the Third of France is
entitled to a high rank. As regards style and treatment Miss Freer has made a great
advance upon her 'Elizabeth de Valois,' as that book was an advance upon her
'Marguerite D'Angoulême.'"—*Spectator.*

"We heartily recommend this work to the reading public. Miss Freer has much, perhaps all, of the quick perception and picturesque style by which Miss Strickland has
earned her well-deserved popularity."—*Critic.*

ELIZABETH DE VALOIS, QUEEN OF SPAIN, AND

THE COURT OF PHILIP II. From numerous unpublished sources in
the Archives of France, Italy, and Spain. By MISS FREER. 2 vols
post 8vo. with fine Portraits by HEATH. 21s.

"It is not attributing too much to Miss Freer to say that herself and Mr. Prescott are
probably the best samples of our modern biographers. The present volumes will be a boon
to posterity for which it will be grateful. Equally suitable for instruction and amusement,
they portray one of the most interesting characters and periods of history."—*John Bull.*

"Such a book as the memoir of Elizabeth de Valois is a literary treasure which will be
the more appreciated as its merits obtain that reputation to which they most justly are
entitled. Miss Freer has done her utmost to make the facts of Elizabeth's, Don Carlos',
and Philip II.'s careers fully known, as they actually transpired."—*Bell's Messenger.*

THE LIFE OF MARGUERITE D'ANGOULEME,

QUEEN of NAVARRE, SISTER of FRANCIS I. By MISS FREER.
Second Edition, 2 vols. with fine Portraits, 21s.

"This is a very useful and amusing book. It is a good work, very well done. The
authoress is quite equal in power and grace to Miss Strickland. She must have spent great
time and labour in collecting the information, which she imparts in an easy and agreeable
manner. It is difficult to lay down her book after having once begun it. This is owing
partly to the interesting nature of the subject, partly to the skilful manner in which it has
been treated. No other life of Marguerite has yet been published, even in France. Indeed,
till Louis Philippe ordered the collection and publication of manuscripts relating to the
history of France, no such work could be published. It is difficult to conceive how, under
any circumstances, it could have been better done."—*Standard.*

LODGE'S PEERAGE AND BARONETAGE FOR 1860.

UNDER THE ESPECIAL PATRONAGE OF HER MAJESTY AND H.R.H. THE PRINCE CONSORT. Corrected throughout by the Nobility. Twenty-Ninth Edition, in 1 vol. royal 8vo., with the Arms beautifully engraved, handsomely bound, with gilt edges, price 31s. 6d.

LODGE'S PEERAGE AND BARONETAGE is acknowledged to be the most complete, as well as the most elegant, work of the kind. As an established and authentic authority on all questions respecting the family histories, honours, and connections of the titled aristocracy, no work has ever stood so high. It is published under the especial patronage of Her Majesty, and His Royal Highness the Prince Consort, and is annually corrected throughout, from the personal communications of the Nobility. It is the only work of its class, in which, *the type being kept constantly standing*, every correction is made in its proper place to the date of publication, an advantage which gives it supremacy over all its competitors. Independently of its full and authentic information respecting the existing Peers and Baronets of the realm, the most sedulous attention is given in its pages to the collateral branches of the various noble families, and the names of many thousand individuals are introduced, which do not appear in other records of the titled classes. For its authority, correctness, and facility of arrangement, and the beauty of its typography and binding, the work is justly entitled to the high place it occupies on the tables of Her Majesty and the Nobility.

" Lodge's Peerage must supersede all other works of the kind, for two reasons ; first, it is on a better plan ; and, secondly, it is better executed. We can safely pronounce it to be the readiest, the most useful, and exactest of modern works on the subject."—*Spectator.*

" A work which corrects all errors of former works. It is the production of a herald, we had almost said, by birth, but certainly by profession and studies, Mr. Lodge, the Norroy King of Arms. It is a most useful publication."—*Times.*

" As perfect a Peerage of the British Empire as we are ever likely to see published. Great pains have been taken to make it as complete and accurate as possible. The work is patronised by Her Majesty and the Prince Consort; and it is worthy of a place in every gentleman's library, as well as in every public institution."—*Herald.*

" As a work of contemporaneous history, this volume is of great value—the materials having been derived from the most authentic sources and in the majority of cases emanating from the noble families themselves. It contains all the needful information respecting the nobility of the Empire."—*Post.*

" This work should form a portion of every gentleman's library. At all times, the information which it contains, derived from official sources exclusively at the command of the author, is of importance to most classes of the community ; to the antiquary it must be invaluable, for implicit reliance may be placed on its contents."—*Globe.*

" This work derives great value from the high authority of Mr. Lodge. The plan is excellent."—*Literary Gazette.*

" When any book has run through so many editions, its reputation is so indelibly stamped, that it requires neither criticism nor praise. It is but just, however, to say, that ' Lodge's Peerage and Baronetage ' is the most elegant and accurate, and the best of its class. The chief point of excellence attaching to this Peerage consists neither in its elegance of type nor its completeness of illustration, but in its authenticity, which is insured by the letter-press being always kept standing, and by immediate alteration being made whenever any change takes place, either by death or otherwise, amongst the nobility of the United Kingdom. The work has obtained the special patronage of Her Most Gracious Majesty, and of His Royal Highness the Prince Consort, which patronage has never been better or more worthily bestowed."—*Messenger.*

" ' Lodge's Peerage and Baronetage' has become, as it were, an 'institution' of this country ; in other words, it is indispensable, and cannot be done without, by any person having business in the great world. The authenticity of this valuable work, as regards the several topics to which it refers, has never been exceeded, and, consequently, it must be received as one of the most important contributions to social and domestic history ex'ant. A book of reference—indispensible in most cases, useful in all—it should be in the hands of every one having connections in, or transactions with, the aristocracy."—*Observer* .

LODGE'S GENEALOGY OF THE PEERAGE AND

BARONETAGE OF THE BRITISH EMPIRE. A NEW AND REVISED EDITION. Uniform with " THE PEERAGE" Volume, with the arms beautifully engraved, handsomely bound with gilt edges, price 31s. 6d.

The desire very generally manifested for a republication of this volume has dictated the present entire revision of its contents. The Armorial Bearings prefixed to the History of each Noble Family, render the work complete in itself and uniform with the Volume of THE PEERAGE, which it is intended to accompany and illustrate. The object of the whole Work, in its two distinct yet combined characters, has been useful and correct information; and the careful attention devoted to this object throughout will, it is hoped, render the Work worthy of the August Patronage with which it is honoured and of the liberal assistance accorded by its Noble Correspondents, and will secure from them and from the Public, the same cordial reception it has hitherto experienced. The great advantage of " The Genealogy" being thus given in a separate volume, Mr. Lodge has himself explained in the Preface to " The Peerage "

EPISODES OF FRENCH HISTORY DURING THE

CONSULATE AND FIRST EMPIRE. By MISS PARDOE, author of " The Life of Marie de Medicis," &c. 2 vols. 21s.

" We recommend Miss Pardoe's ' Episodes' as very pleasant reading. They cannot fail to entertain and instruct."—*Critic.*
" One of the most amusing and instructive books Miss Pardoe has ever given to the public."—*Messenger.*
" In this lively and agreeable book Miss Pardoe gives a fair picture of the society of the times, which has never been treated in a more interesting and pleasant manner."— *Chronicle.*

THE LIFE AND TIMES OF GEORGE VILLIERS,

DUKE OF BUCKINGHAM. By MRS. THOMSON, Author of " The Life of the Duchess of Marlborough," " Memoirs of Sir W. Raleigh," &c. With Portrait. (*Just Ready.*)

THE LIVES OF PHILIP HOWARD, EARL OF

ARUNDEL, AND OF ANNE DACRES, HIS WIFE. Edited from the Original MSS, By the DUKE OF NORFOLK, E.M. 1 vol. antique.

" These biographies will be read with interest. They throw valuable light on the social habits and the prevalent feelings of the Elizabethan age."—*Literary Gazette.*

MEMOIRS OF BERANGER. WRITTEN BY HIM-

SELF. ENGLISH COPYRIGHT EDITION. Second Edition, with numerous Additional Anecdotes and Notes, hitherto unpublished. 8vo. with Portrait.

" This is the Copyright Translation of Béranger's Biography. It appears in a handsome volume, and is worthy of all praise as an honest piece of work. In this account of his life, the Poet displays all the mingled gaiety and earnestness, the warm-hearted sincerity, inseparable from his character. He tells, with an exquisite simplicity, the story of his early years. His life, he says, is the fairest commentary on his songs, therefore he writes it. The charm of the narrative is altogether fresh. It includes a variety of *chansons*, now first printed, touching closely on the personal history of which they form a part, shrewd sayings, and, as the field of action in life widens, many sketches of contemporaries, and free judgments upon men and things. There is a full appendix to the Memoir, rich in letters hitherto unpublished, and in information which completes the story of Béranger's life. The book should be read by all."—*Examiner.*

THE BOOK OF ORDERS OF KNIGHTHOOD, AND

DECORATIONS OF HONOUR OF ALL NATIONS; COMPRISING AN HISTORICAL ACCOUNT OF EACH ORDER, MILITARY, NAVAL AND CIVIL; with Lists of the Knights and Companions of each British Order. EMBELLISHED WITH FIVE HUNDRED FAC-SIMILE COLOURED ILLUSTRATIONS OF THE INSIGNIA OF THE VARIOUS ORDERS. Edited by SIR BERNARD BURKE, Ulster King of Arms. 1 vol. royal 8vo., handsomely bound, with gilt edges, price £2. 2s.

"This valuable and attractive work may claim the merit of being the best of its kind. It is so comprehensive in its character, and so elegant in its style, that it far outstrips all competitors. A full historical account of the orders of every country is given, with lists of the Knights and Companions of each British Order. Among the most attractive features of the work are the illustrations. They are numerous and beautiful, highly coloured, and giving an exact representation of the different decorations. The origin of each Order, the rules and regulations, and the duties incumbent on its members, are all given at full length. The fact of the work being under the supervision of Sir Bernard Burke, and endorsed by his authority, gives it another recommendation to the public favour."—*Sun*

"This is, indeed, a splendid book. It is an uncommon combination of a library book of reference and a book for a boudoir, undoubtedly uniting beauty and utility. It gives a sketch of the foundation and history of all recognised decorations of honour, among all nations, arranged in alphabetical order. The fac-smiles of the insignia are well drawn and coloured, and present a brilliant effect. Sir Bernard Burke has done his work well; and this book of the quintessence of the aristocracy will soon find its place in every library and drawing-room."—.*Globe*

JOURNAL OF AN ENGLISH OFFICER IN INDIA.

By MAJOR NORTH, 60th Rifles, Deputy Judge Advocate-General, and Aide-de-Camp to General Havelock. 1 vol. with portrait.

"We must commend Major's North's 'Journal' to universal approbation. It is manly in tone, noble in expression, and full of feeling, alike honourable to the soldier and and gallant profession. When we state that the book tells of the progress of the lion-hearted Havelock's little band which relieved Lucknow, and is the first faithful record of the deeds of arms performed by that phalanx of heroes, we have said enough to cause it to be read, we are convinced, by every person who can avail himself of the opportunity of learning what were the hardships of his countrymen, and how immense were the sacrifices they made to save the English besieged inhabitants from a repetition of the atrocities of Cawnpore. We have as yet seen no book connected with the Indian mutiny which has given us so much gratification as Major North's Journal."—*Messenger.*

EASTERN HOSPITALS AND ENGLISH NURSES;

The Narrative of Twelve Months' Experience in the Hospitals of Koulali and Scutari. By A LADY VOLUNTEER. Third and Cheaper Edition, 1 vol. post 8vo. with Illustrations, 6s. bound.

"The story of the noble deeds done by Miss Nightingale and her devoted sisterhood will never be more effectively told than in the beautiful narrative contained in these volumes."—*John Bull.*

PICTURES OF SPORTING LIFE AND CHARACTER.

By LORD WILLIAM LENNOX. 2 vols. with Illustrations. 21s.

"This work may be characterised as a perfect synopsis of English sports in the 19th century. Were the whole of the books previously written on the subject destroyed, Lord William Lennox's alone would preserve a lifelike picture of the sports and amusements of our age. The volumes will be read with intense enjoyment by multitudes, for their author is an accomplished *littérateur*, who has known how to vary his theme so skilfully and to intersperse it with so many anecdotes and personal recollections of England's most distinguished men, that even those who are not themselves given to sport will be deeply interested in the light he throws upon English society."—*Illustrated News of the World.*

THE COUNTESS OF BONNEVAL: HER LIFE AND

LETTERS. By LADY GEORGIANA FULLERTON. 2 vols. 21s.

" The whole work forms one of those touching stories which create a lasting impression."—*Athenæum.*

" The life of the Count de Bonneval is a page in history, but it reads like a romance ; that of the Countess, removed from war and politics, never oversteps the domestic sphere, yet is equally romantic and singular. An accomplished writer has taken up the threads of this modest life, and brought out her true character in a very interesting and animated memoir. The story of the Countess of Bonneval is related with the happy art and grace which so characterise the author."—*U. S. Magazine.*

THE LIFE OF MARIE DE MEDICIS, QUEEN OF

FRANCE, CONSORT OF HENRY IV., AND REGENT UNDER LOUIS XIII. By MISS PARDOE. Second Edition. 3 vols. 8vo. Portraits.

MEMOIRS OF THE BARONESS D'OBERKIRCH,

ILLUSTRATIVE OF THE SECRET HISTORY OF THE COURTS OF FRANCE, RUSSIA, AND GERMANY. WRITTEN BY HERSELF, and Edited by Her Grandson, the COUNT DE MONTBRISON. 3 vols. post 8vo. 15s.

" The Baroness d'Oberkirch being the intimate friend of the Empress of Russia, wife of Paul I., and the confidential companion of the Duchess of Bourbon, her facilities for obtaining information respecting the most private affairs of the principal Courts of Europe, render her Memoirs unrivalled as a book of interesting anecdotes of the royal, noble and other celebrated individuals who flourished on the continent during the latter part of the last century. The volumes form a valuable addition to the personal history of an important period. They deserve general popularity."—*Daily News.*

MEMOIRS OF RACHEL. 2 vols. with Portrait. 21s.

"A book sure to attract public attention, and well meriting it."—*Globe.*

SCOTTISH HEROES IN THE DAYS OF WALLACE

AND BRUCE. By the REV. A. LOW, A.M. 2 vols. post 8vo.

MEMOIRS AND CORRESPONDENCE OF MAJOR

GENERAL SIR W. NOTT, G.C.B., COMMANDER OF THE ARMY OF CANDAHAR, AND ENVOY AT THE COURT OF LUCKNOW. 2 vols. 8vo. with Portrait. 16s. bound.

RULE AND MISRULE OF THE ENGLISH IN

AMERICA. By the Author of "SAM SLICK." 2 vols. post 8vo.

" We conceive this work to be by far the most valuable and important Judge Haliburton has ever written. While teeming with interest, moral and historical, to the general reader, it equally constitutes a philosophical study for the politician and statesman. It will be found to let in a flood of light upon the actual origin, formation, and progress of the republic of the United States."—*Naval and Military Gazette.*

RECOLLECTIONS OF WEST END LIFE; WITH

SKETCHES OF SOCIETY IN PARIS, INDIA, &c. By MAJOR CHAMBRE late 17th Lancers. 2 vols. with Portrait of George IV.

" We find in Major Chambre's lively sketches a mass of amusing anecdotes relating to persons eminent in their day for their position, wit, and political reputation. All that relates to George IV. will be read with attention and interest."—*Messenger.*

THE UPPER and LOWER AMOOR; A NARRATIVE

OF TRAVEL AND ADVENTURE. By T. W. ATKINSON. Author of "ORIENTAL and WESTERN SIBERIA." With Map and numerous Illustrations. *(In the Press.)*

SIXTEEN YEARS OF AN ARTIST'S LIFE IN

MOROCCO, SPAIN, AND THE CANARY ISLANDS. By MRS. ELIZABETH MURRAY. 2 vols. 8vo. with Coloured Illustrations.

"Mrs. Murray, wife, we believe, of the English Consul at Teneriffe, is one of the first of female English Water Colour Artists. She draws well, and her colour is bright, pure, transparent, and sparkling. Her book is like her painting, luminous, rich and fresh. We welcome it (as the public will also do) with sincere pleasure. It is a hearty book, written by a clever, quick-sighted, and thoughtful woman, who, slipping a steel pen on the end of her brush, thus doubly armed, uses one end as well as the other, being with both a bright colourer, and accurate describer of colours, outlines, sensations, landscapes and things. In a word, Mrs. Murray is a clever artist, who writes forcibly and agreeably."—*Athenæum.*

"Mrs. Elizabeth Murray is known to the artistic world as the principal star of the Female Exhibition of Paintings. She left England as she tells us, at eighteen, with all the hopes and aspirations of an artist before her. At Morocco she becomes the wife of a gentleman who is successively Consul at Tangiers and Teneriffe. She has, in consequence, peculiar advantages for the observation of Moorish and Spanish society, and as she possesses great observation and wields the pen as cleverly as the pencil, she has produced a book not only of interest, but of importance. In every way, whether descriptive or anecdotal, the work claims to be placed amongst the very best works of travel in the English Language."—*Chronicle.*

REVELATIONS OF PRISON LIFE; WITH AN EN-

QUIRY INTO PRISON DISCIPLINE AND SECONDARY PUNISHMENTS. By GEORGE LAVAL CHESTERTON, 25 Years Governor of the House of Correction at Cold-Bath Fields. Third Edition, Revised. 1 vol.

"Mr. Chesterton has had a rare experience of human frailty. He has lived with the felon, the forger, the *lorette*, the vagabond, the murderer; has looked into the darkest sepulchres of the heart, without finding reason to despair of mankind. In his belief the worst of men have still some of the angel left. Such a testimony from such a quarter is full of novelty as it is of interest. As a curious bit of human history these volumes are remarkable. They are very real, very simple; dramatic without exaggeration, philosophic without being dull."—*Athenæum.*

THE OLD COURT SUBURB; OR, MEMORIALS OF

KENSINGTON; REGAL, CRITICAL, AND ANECDOTICAL. By LEIGH HUNT. Second Edition. 2 vols. post 8vo.

"A delightful book. It will be welcome to all readers, and most welcome to those who have a love for the best kinds of reading."—*Examiner.*

MY EXILE. BY ALEXANDER HERZEN. 2 vols.

"Mr. Herzen's narrative, ably and unaffectedly written, and undoubtedly authentic, is indeed superior in interest to nine-tenths of the existing works on Russia."—*Athenæum.*

A PRACTICAL GUIDE IN OBTAINING PROBATES,

ADMINISTRATIONS, &c., in Her Majesty's Court of Probate; with numerous Precedents. By EDWARD WEATHERLY, of Doctor's Commons. Dedicated, by permission, to the Right Hon. Sir CRESSWELL CRESSWELL, Judge of the New Court of Probate. Cheaper Edition. 12s

'A most valuable book. Its contents are very diversified—meeting almost every use."—*Solicitor's Journal.*

ORIENTAL AND WESTERN SIBERIA; A NAR-

RATIVE OF SEVEN YEARS' EXPLORATIONS AND ADVENTURES IN SIBERIA, MONGOLIA, THE KIRGHIS STEPPES, CHINESE TARTARY, AND CENTRAL ASIA. By THOMAS WITLAM ATKINSON. In one large volume, royal 8vo., Price £2. 2s., elegantly bound. Embellished with upwards of 50 Illustrations, including numerous beautifully coloured plates, from drawings by the Author, and a map.

"By virtue alike of its text and its pictures, we place this book of travel in the first rank among those illustrated gift-books now so much sought by the public. Mr. Atkinson's book is most readable. The geographer finds in it notice of ground heretofore left undescribed, the ethnologist, geologist, and botanist, find notes and pictures, too, of which they know the value, the sportman's taste is gratified by chronicles of sport, the lover of adventure will find a number of perils and escapes to hang over, and the lover of a frank good-humoured way of speech will find the book a pleasant one in every page. Seven years of wandering, thirty-nine thousand five hundred miles of moving to and fro in a wild and almost unknown country, should yield a book worth reading, and they do."—*Examiner.*

"A book of travels which in value and sterling interest must take rank as a landmark in geographical literature. Its coloured illustrations and wood engravings are of a high order, and add a great charm to the narrative. Mr. Atkinson has travelled where it is believed no European has been before. He has seen nature in the wildest, sublimest, and also the most beautiful aspects the old world can present. These he has depicted by pen and pencil. He has done both well. Many a fireside will rejoice in the determination which converted the artist into an author. Mr. Atkinson is a thorough Englishman, brave and accomplished, a lover of adventure and sport of every kind. He knows enough of mineralogy, geology, and botany to impart a scientific interest to his descriptions and drawings; possessing a keen sense of humour, he tells many a racy story. The sportsman and the lover of adventure, whether by flood or field, will find ample stores in the stirring tales of his interesting travels."—*Daily News.*

"An animated and intelligent narrative, appreciably enriching the literature of English travel. Mr. Atkinson's sketches were made by express permission of the late Emperor of Russia. Perhaps no English artist was ever before admitted into this enchanted land of history, or provided with the talisman and amulet of a general passport; and well has Mr. Atkinson availed himself of the privilege. Our extracts will have served to illustrate the originality and variety of Mr. Atkinson's observations and adventures during his protracted wanderings of nearly forty thousand miles. Mr. Atkinson's pencil was never idle, and he has certainly brought home with him the forms, and colours, and other characteristics of a most extraordinary diversity of groups and scenes. As a sportsman Mr. Atkinson enjoyed a plenitude of excitement. His narrative is well stored with incidents of adventure. His ascent of the Bielouka is a chapter of the most vivid romance of travel, yet it is less attractive than his relations of wanderings across the Desert of Gobi and up the Tangnou Chain."—*Athenæum.*

"We predict that Mr. Atkinson's 'Siberia' will very often assume the shape of a Christmas Present or New Year's Gift, as it possesses, in an eminent degree, four very precious and suitable qualities for that purpose,—namely, usefulness, elegance, instruction and novelty. It is a work of great value, not merely on account of its splendid illustrations, but for the amount it contains of authentic and highly interesting intelligence concerning regions which, in all probability, has never, previous to Mr. Atkinson's explorations, been visited by an European. Mr. Atkinson's adventures are told in a manly style. The valuable and interesting information the book contains, gathered at a vast expense, is lucidly arranged, and altogether the work is one that the author-artist may well be proud of, and with which those who study it cannot fail to be delighted."—*John Bull.*

"To the geographer, the geologist, the ethnographer, the sportsman, and to those who read only for amusement, this will be an acceptable volume. Mr. Atkinson is not only an adventurous traveller, but a correct and amusing writer."—*Literary Gazette.*

TRAVELS IN EASTERN AFRICA, WITH THE
NARRATIVE OF A RESIDENCE IN MOZAMBIQUE: 1856 to 1859.
By LYONS McLEOD, Esq. F.R.G.S.. &c. Late British Consul in Mo-
zambique. 2 vols. With Map and Illustrations.

A JOURNEY ON A PLANK FROM KIEV TO EAUX-
BONNES. By LADY CHARLOTTE PEPYS. 2 vols, with Illustrations. 21s. (*Just Ready*).

LAKE NGAMI; OR EXPLORATIONS AND DIS-
COVERIES DURING FOUR YEARS' WANDERINGS IN THE WILDS OF
SOUTH-WESTERN AFRICA. By CHARLES JOHN ANDERSSON. 1 vol.
royal 8vo., with Map and upwards of 50 Illustrations, representing Sporting Adventures, Subjects of Natural History, &c. Second Edition.

"This narrative of African explorations and discoveries is one of the most important
geographical works that have lately appeared. It contains the account of two journeys
made between the years 1850 and 1854, in the first of which the countries of the Damaras
and the Ovambo, previously scarcely known in Europe, were explored; and in the second
the newly-discovered Lake Ngami was reached by a route that had been deemed imprac-
ticable, but which proves to be the shortest and the best. The work contains much scientific
and accurate information as to the geology, the scenery, products, and resources of the
regions explored, with notices of the religion, manners, and customs of the native tribes.
The continual sporting adventures, and other remarkable occurrences, intermingled with
the narrative of travel, make the book as interesting to read as a romance, as, indeed, a
good book of travels ought always to be. The illustrations by Wolf are admirably designed,
and most of them represent scenes as striking as any witnessed by Jules Gérard or Gordon
Cumming."—*Literary Gazette.*

THE OXONIAN IN THELEMARKEN; OR, NOTES
OF TRAVEL IN SOUTH-WESTERN NORWAY, WITH GLANCES AT THE
LEGENDARY LORE OF THAT DISTRICT. By the Rev. F. METCALFE
M.A., Fellow of Lincoln College. 2 vols. with illustrations.

"This new book is as lively as its predecessor, its matter is as good, or better. The
intermixture of legends and traditions with the notes of travel adds to the real value of the
work, and strengthens its claim on a public that desires to be amused."—*Examiner.*

THE OXONIAN IN NORWAY; OR, NOTES OF
EXCURSIONS IN THAT COUNTRY. By the Rev. F. METCALFE, M.A.,
Fellow of Lincoln College, Oxford. New and Cheaper Edition, revised,
1 vol. post 8vo., with Map and additional Illustrations.

"Mr. Metcalfe's book is as full of facts and interesting information as it can hold, and
is interlarded with racy anecdotes. Some of these are highly original and entertaining.
More than this, it is a truly valuable work, containing a fund of information on the statistics,
politics, and religion of the countries visited."—*Blackwood's Magazine.*

SIX YEARS IN RUSSIA. BY AN ENGLISH LADY.
2 vols. post 8vo. with Illustrations. 21s. bound.

A SUMMER AND WINTER IN THE TWO SICILIES.

By JULIA KAVANAGH, Author of " Nathalie," " Adèle," &c. 2 vols. post 8vo. with illustrations, 21s. bound.

"Miss Kavanagh is a woman of genius and imagination. She has a graceful and brilliant pen, much observation of character, and a keen eye for the aspects of nature. Her volumes contain much that is new. They are among the pleasantest volumes of travel we have lately met with, and we can cordially recommend them. Readers will find in these volumes the glow and colour of Italian skies, the rich and passionate beauty of Italian scenery, and the fresh simplicity of Southern life touched by the hand of an artist, and described by the perceptions of a warm-hearted and sympathizing woman."—*The Press.*

THE JEWS IN THE EAST. BY THE REV. P.

BEATON, M.A. From the German of DR. FRANKL. 2 vols. 21s.

" Those persons who are curious in matters connected with Jerusalem and its inhabitants, are strongly recommended to read this work, which contains more information than is to be found in a dozen of the usual books of travel."—*Times.*

"This book will richly reward perusal. We cordially recommend the narrative for solid information given from an unusual point of view, for power of description, for incident, and for details of manners, domestic habits, traditions, &c.,"—*Globe.*

"A very interesting work, one of the most original books of modern travel, that we have encountered for a long time."—*John Bull.*

CHOW-CHOW; BEING SELECTIONS FROM A JOUR-

NAL KEPT IN INDIA, &c. By the VISCOUNTESS FALKLAND. New and Revised Edition, 2 vols. 8vo., with Illustrations. 21s.

"Lady Falkland's work may be read with interest and pleasure, and the reader will rise from the perusal instructed as well as amused."—*Athenæum.*

A PERSONAL NARRATIVE OF THE DISCOVERY

OF THE NORTH-WEST PASSAGE with Numerous Incidents of Travel and Adventure during nearly Five Years' Continuous Service in the Arctic Regions while in Search of the Expedition under Sir John Franklin. By ALEX. ARMSTRONG, M.D., R.N., late Surgeon and Naturalist of H.M.S 'Investigator.' 1 vol. With Map and Plate, 16s.

"This book is sure to take a prominent position in every library in which works of discovery and adventure are to be met with."—*Daily News.*

THE WANDERER IN ARABIA. BY G. T. LOWTH,

ESQ. 2 vols. post 8vo. with Illustrations. 12s.

"Mr. Lowth has shown himself in these volumes to be an intelligent traveller, a keen observer of nature, and an accomplished artist."—*Post.*

SPORTING ADVENTURES IN THE NEW WORLD;

OR, DAYS AND NIGHTS OF MOOSE HUNTING IN THE PINE FORESTS OF ACADIA. By CAMPBELL HARDY, ROYAL ARTILLERY. 2 vols. post 8vo. with illustrations. 12s.

"A spirited record of sporting adventures, very entertaining and well worthy the attention of all sportsmen who desire some fresher field than Europe can afford them."—*Press.*

A PILGRIMAGE INTO DAUPHINE; WITH A VISIT

TO THE MONASTERY OF THE GRANDE CHARTREUSE, AND ANECDOTES, INCIDENTS, AND SKETCHES FROM TWENTY DEPARTMENTS OF FRANCE. By the REV. G. M. MUSGRAVE, A.M. 2 vols. with Illustrations.

FAMILY ROMANCE; OR, DOMESTIC ANNALS OF
THE ARISTOCRACY. BY SIR BERNARD BURKE. ULSTER KING OF
ARMS. 2 vols. post 8vo. 21s.

Among the many other interesting legends and romantic family histories comprised in these volumes, will be found the following :—The wonderful narrative of Maria Stella, Lady Newborough, who claimed on such strong evidence to be a Princess of the House of Orleans. and disputed the identity of Louis Philippe— The story of the humble marriage of the beautiful Countess of Strathmore, and the sufferings and fate of her only child—The Leaders of Fashion, from Grammont to D'Orsay—The rise of the celebrated Baron Ward, now Prime Minister at Parma—The curious claim to the Earldom of Crawford—The Strange Vicissitudes of our Great Families, replete with the most romantic details—The story of the Kirkpatricks of Closeburn (the ancestors of the French Empress), and the remarkable tradition associated with them—The Legend of the Lambtons—The verification in our own time of the famous prediction as to the Earls of Mar— Lady Ogilvy's escape—The Beresford and Wynyard ghost stories, &c.

"It were impossible to praise too highly as a work of amusement these two most interesting volumes, whether we should have regard to its excellent plan or its not less excellent execution. The volumes are just what ought to be found on every drawing-room table. Here you have nearly fifty captivating romances with the pith of all their interest preserved in undiminished poignancy, and any one may be read in half an hour. It is not the least of their merits that the romances are founded on fact—or what, at least, has been handed down for truth by long tradition—and the romance of reality far exceeds the romance of fiction. Each story is told in the clear, unaffected style with which the author's former works have made the public familiar."—*Standard.*

THE ROMANCE OF THE FORUM; OR, NARRA-
TIVES, SCENES, AND ANECDOTES FROM COURTS OF JUSTICE.
SECOND SERIES. BY PETER BURKE, ESQ., of the Inner Temple
Barrister-at-Law. 2 vols. post 8vo. 12s.

PRINCIPAL CONTENTS :—Lord Crichton's Revenge—The Great Douglas Cause—Lord and Lady Kinnaird—Marie Delorme and Her Husband—The Spectral Treasure—Murders in Inns of Court—Matthieson the Forger—Trials that established the Illegality of Slavery—The Lover Highwayman—The Accusing Spirit—The Attorney-General of the Reign of Terror—Eccentric Occurrences in the Law—Adventuresses of Pretended Rank—The Courier of Lyons—General Sarrazin's Bigamy—The Elstree Murder—Count Bocarmé and his wife—Professor Webster, &c.

"The favour with which the first series of this publication was received, has induced Mr. Burke to extend his researches, which he has done with great judgment. The incidents forming the subject of the second series are as extraordinary in every respect, as those which obtained so high a meed of celebrity for the first."—*Messenger.*

THE MAN OF THE PEOPLE.   BY WILLIAM
HOWITT. 3 vols. post 8vo. (*Just Ready*).

SONGS OF THE CAVALIERS AND ROUNDHEADS,
JACOBITE BALLADS, &c. By G. W. THORNBURY. 1 vol. with
numerous Illustrations by H. S. MARKS. Elegantly bound. 6s.

"Mr. Thornbury has produced a volume of songs and ballads worthy to rank with Macaulay's or Aytoun's Lays."—*Chronicle.* "Those who love picture, life, and costume in song will here find what they love."—*Athenæum.*

POEMS. BY THE AUTHOR OF " JOHN HALIFAX,

GENTLEMAN," " A WOMAN'S THOUGHTS ABOUT WOMEN," &c.
1 vol. with Illustrations by BIRKET FOSTER. 10s. 6d. bound.

" A volume of poems which will assuredly take its place with those of Goldsmith, Gray.
and Cowper, on the favourite shelf of every Englishman's library. We discover in these
poems all the firmness, vigour, and delicacy of touch which characterise the author's prose
works, and in addition, an ineffable tenderness and grace, such as we find in few poetical
compositions besides those of Tennyson."—*Illustrated News of the World.*

" We are well pleased with these poems by our popular novelist. They are the expression
of genuine thoughts, feelings, and aspirations, and the expression is almost always graceful, musical and well-coloured. A high, pure tone of morality pervades each set of verses,
and each strikes the reader as inspired by some real event, or condition of mind, and not by
some idle fancy or fleeting sentiment."—*Spectator.*

A LIFE FOR A LIFE. BY THE AUTHOR OF

" JOHN HALIFAX GENTLEMAN," &c.

" In 'A Life for a Life' the author is fortunate in a good subject, and she has produced a
work of strong effect. The reader, having read the book through for the story, will be apt
(if he be of our persuasion) to return and read again many pages and passages with greater
pleasure than on a first perusal. The whole book is replete with a graceful, tender delicacy ;
and, in addition to its other merits, it is written in good, careful English."—*Athenæum.*

" This book is signally the best its author has yet produced. The interest is intense,
and is everywhere admirably sustained. Incident abounds, and both dialogue and style are
natural and flowing. Great delicacy in the development of character, and a subtle power of
self-analysis are conspicuous in 'A Life for a Life,' while the purity of its religious views,
and the elevation—the grandeur, indeed—of its dominating sentiments, render its influences
in every sense healthy and invigorating."—*The Press.*

" 'A Life for a Life' is one of the best of the author's works. We like it better than
'John Halifax.' It is a book we should like every member of every family in England to
read."—*Herald.*

REALITIES OF PARIS LIFE. BY THE AUTHOR

OF " FLEMISH INTERIORS," &c. 3 vols. with Illustrations. 31s. 6d.

" 'Realities of Paris Life' is a good addition to Paris books, and important as affording
true and sober pictures of the Paris poor."—*Athenæum.*

" There is much new matter pleasantly put together in these volumes. Their merit will
commend itself to all readers."—*Examiner.*

NOVELS AND NOVELISTS, FROM ELIZABETH TO

VICTORIA. By J. C. JEAFFRESON, Esq. 2 vols. with Portraits. 21s.

THE RIDES AND REVERIES OF MR. ÆSOP SMITH.

By MARTIN F. TUPPER, D.C.L., F.R.S., Author of " Proverbial Philosophy," " Stephen Langton," &c., 1 vol. post 8vo.

" This work will do good service to Mr. Tupper's literary reputation It combines
with lucidity and acuteness of judgment, freshness of fancy and elegance of sentiment. In
its cheerful and instructive pages sound moral principles are forcibly inculcated, and every-
day truths acquire an air of novelty, and are rendered peculiarly attractive by being expressed
in that epigrammatic language which so largely contributed to the popularity of the author's
former work, entitled ' Proverbial Philosophy.' "—*Morning Post.*

A MOTHER'S TRIAL. BY THE AUTHOR OF

" THE DISCIPLINE OF LIFE," " THE TWO BROTHERS," &c. 1 vol.
with Illustrations, by BIRKET FOSTER. 7s. 6d. bound.

" 'A Mother's Trial,' by Lady Emily Ponsonby, is a work we can recommend. It
breathes purity and refinement in every page."—*Leader.*

SEVEN YEARS.

By JULIA KAVANAGH,
Author of " NATHALIE," 3 vols.

" Nothing can be better of its kind than
Miss Kavanagh's ' Seven Years.' The
story never flags in interest, so life-like
are the characters that move in it, so
natural the incidents, and so genuine the
emotions they excite in persons who have
taken fast hold on our sympathy."—
Spectator.

LUCY CROFTON.

By the Author of " MARGARET MAIT-
LAND." 1 vol.

" This is a charming novel. The characters are excellent; the plot is well
defined and new; and the interest is kept
up with an intensity which is seldom
met with in these days. The author deserves our thanks for one of the most
pleasant books of the season."—*Herald.*

THE WOOD-RANGERS.

By CAPTAIN MAYNE REID.

From the French of Louis de Bellemare.
3 vols., with illustrations.

THE LITTLE BEAUTY.

By MRS. GREY,
Author of " THE GAMBLER'S WIFE." 3 v.

MR. AND MRS. ASHETON.

By the Author of " MARGARET AND HER
BRIDESMAIDS." 3 vols.

THE WAY OF THE WORLD.

By ALISON REED. 3 vols.

" There is a spell and fascination upon
one from the first page to the last."—
John Bull.

ALMOST A HEROINE.

By the Author of " CHARLES AUCHES-
TER," &c. 3 vols.

" This novel is the author's best."—
Herald.

WAIT AND HOPE.

By JOHN EDMUND READE. 3 vols.

" ' Wait and Hope' reminds us of the
style of Godwin."—*Athenæum.*

RAISED TO THE PEERAGE.

By MRS. OCTAVIUS OWEN. 3 vols.

" ' Raised to the Peerage' possesses very
many of the requisites of a really good
novel."—*Examiner.*

FEMALE INFLUENCE.

By LADY CHARLOTTE PEPYS, 2 vols.

LETHELIER.

By E. HENEAGE DERING, Esq.
2 vols.

THE QUEEN OF HEARTS.

By WILKIE COLLINS. 3 vols.

" ' The Queen of Hearts' is such a fascinating creature that we cannot choose but
follow her through the pages with something of a lover's tenderness. As for the
three old men, they are as good in their
way as the Brothers Cheeryble of immor-
tal memory."—*Literary Gazette.*

STEPHAN LANGTON.

By MARTIN. F. TUPPER. D.C.L. F.R.S.
Author of " PROVERBIAL PHILOSOPHY."
&c., 2 vols. with fine engravings.

" These volumes are pre-eminently qualified to attract attention both from their
peculiar style and their great ability. The
author has long been celebrated for his
attainments in literary creation, but the
present work is incomparably superior to
anything he has hitherto produced.—*Sun*

CREEDS.

By the Author of " THE MORALS OF
MAY FAIR." 3 vols.

" This is a novel of strong dramatic
situation, powerful plot, alluring and continuous interest, admirably defined
characters, and much excellent remark
upon human motives and social positions."
—*Literary Gazette.*

THE LEES OF BLENDON HALL.

By the Author of " ALICE WENTWORTH."

" A powerful and well-sustained story of
strong interest."—*Athenæum.*

NEWTON DOGVANE.

A Story of English Life.
By FRANCIS FRANCIS.
With Illustrations by LEECH. 3 vols.

" A capital sporting novel."—*Chronicle.*

HELEN LINDSAY;

Or, THE TRIAL OF FAITH.
By A CLERGYMAN'S DAUGHTER. 2 vols.

WOODLEIGH.

By the Author of " WILDFLOWER,"
"ONE AND TWENTY," &c. 3 vols.

BENTLEY PRIORY.

By MRS. HASTINGS PARKER. 3 vols.

" An acquisition to novel-readers from
its brilliant descriptions, sparkling style,
and interesting story."—*Sun.*

HURST AND BLACKETT'S STANDARD LIBRARY
OF CHEAP EDITIONS OF
POPULAR MODERN WORKS.

Each in a single volume, elegantly printed, bound, and illustrated, price 5s.
A volume to appear every two months. The following are now ready.

VOL. I.—SAM SLICK'S NATURE AND HUMAN NATURE.
ILLUSTRATED BY LEECH.

" The first volume of Messrs. Hurst and Blackett's Standard Library of Cheap Editions of Popular Modern Works forms a very good beginning to what will doubtless be a very successful undertaking. 'Nature and Human Nature' is one of the best of Sam Slick's witty and humorous productions, and well entitled to the large circulation which it cannot fail to obtain in its present convenient and cheap shape. The volume combines with the great recommendations of a clear, bold type, and good paper, the lesser, but still attractive merits, of being well illustrated and elegantly bound."—*Morning Post.*

"This new and cheap edition of Sam Slick's popular work will be an acquisition to all lovers of wit and humour. Mr. Justice Haliburton's writings are so well known to the English public that no commendation is needed. The volume is very handsomely bound and illustrated, and the paper and type are excellent. It is in every way suited for a library edition, and as the names of Messrs. Hurst and Blackett, warrant the character of the works to be produced in their Standard Library, we have no doubt the project will be eminently successful."—*Sun.*

VOL. II.—JOHN HALIFAX, GENTLEMAN.

" This is a very good and a very interesting work. It is designed to trace the career from boyhood to age of a perfect man—a Christian gentleman, and it abounds in incident both well and highly wrought. Throughout it is conceived in a high spirit, and written with great ability, better than any former work, we think, of its deservedly successful author. This cheap and handsome new edition is worthy to pass freely from hand to hand, as a gift book in many households."—*Examiner.*

" The new and cheaper edition of this interesting work will doubtless meet with great success. John Halifax, the hero of this most beautiful story, is no ordinary hero, and this, his history, is no ordinary book. It is a full-length portrait of a true gentleman, one of nature's own nobility. It is also the history of a home and a thoroughly English one. The work abounds in incident, and many of the scenes are full of graphic power and true pathos. It is a book that few will read without becoming wiser and better."—*Scotsman.*

VOL. III.—THE CRESCENT AND THE CROSS.
BY ELIOT WARBURTON.

"Independent of its value as an original narrative, and its useful and interesting information, this work is remarkable for the colouring power and play of fancy with which its descriptions are enlivened. Among its greatest and most lasting charms is its reverent and serious spirit."—*Quarterly Review*

"A book calculated to prove more practically useful was never penned than 'The Crescent and the Cross'—a work which surpasses all others in its homage for the sublime and its love for the beautiful in those famous regions consecrated to everlasting immortality in the annals of the prophets, and which no other writer has ever depicted with a pencil at once so reverent and so picturesque."—*Sun.*

VOL. IV.—NATHALIE. BY JULIA KAVANAGH.

"'Nathalie' is Miss Kavanagh's best imaginative effort. Its manner is gracious and attractive. Its matter is good. A sentiment, a tenderness, are commanded by her which are as individual as they are elegant. We should not soon come to an end were we to specify all the delicate touches and attractive pictures which place 'Nathalie' high among books of its class."—*Athenæum.*

"A tale of untiring interest, full of deep touches of human nature. We have no hesitation in predicting for this delightful tale a lasting popularity, and a place in the foremost ranks of that most instructive kind of fiction—the moral novel."—*John Bull.*

"A more judicious selection than 'Nathalie' could not have been made for Messrs. Hurst and Blackett's Standard Library. The series as it advances realises our first impression, that it will be one of lasting celebrity."—*Literary Gazette.*

[FOR OTHER VOLUMES SEE NEXT PAGE.]

HURST AND BLACKETT'S STANDARD LIBRARY
OF CHEAP EDITIONS.

Each in a single volume, elegantly printed, bound. and illustrated, price 5s.

(CONTINUED).

VOL. V.—A WOMAN'S THOUGHTS ABOUT WOMEN.

BY THE AUTHOR OF "JOHN HALIFAX, GENTLEMAN."

"A book of sound counsel. It is one of the most sensible works of its kind, well-written, true-hearted, and altogether practical. Whoever wishes to give advice to a young lady may thank the author for means of doing so."—*Examiner.*

"The author of 'John Halifax' will retain and extend her hold upon the reading and reasonable public by the merits of her present work, which bears the stamp of good sense and genial feeling."—*Guardian.*

"T ese thoughts are good and humane. They are thoughts we would wish women to think."—*Athenæum*

"This really valuable volume ought to be in every young woman's hand. It will teach her how to think and how to act. We are glad to see it in this Standard Library."—*Literary Gazette.*

VOL. VI.—ADAM GRAEME, OF MOSSGRAY.

BY THE AUTHOR OF "MRS. MARGARET MAITLAND."

"'Adam Graeme' is a story awakening genuine emotions of interest and delight by its admirable pictures of Scottish life and scenery. The plot is cleverly complicated, and there is great vitality in the dialogue, and remarkable brilliancy in the descriptive passages, as who that has read 'Margaret Maitland' would not be prepared to expect? But the story has a 'mightier magnet still,' in the healthy tone which pervades it, in its feminine delicacy of thought and diction, and in the truly womanly tenderness of its sentiments. The eloquent author sets before us the essential attributes of Christian virtue, their deep and silent workings in the heart, and their beautiful manifestations in the life, with a delicacy, a power, and a truth which can hardly be surpassed."—*Morning Post.*

"'Adam Graeme' is full of eloquent writing and description. It is an uncommon work, not only in the power of the style, in the interest of the narrative, and in the delineation of character, but in the lessons it teaches."—*Sun.*

VOL. VII.—SAM SLICK'S WISE SAWS
AND MODERN INSTANCES.

"The best of all Judge Haliburton's admirable works. It is one of the pleasantest books we ever read, and we earnestly recommend it."—*Standard.*

"'The humour of Sam Slick is inexhaustible. He is ever and everywhere a welcome visitor; smiles greet his approach, and wit and wisdom hang upon his tongue. The present production is remarkable alike for its racy humour, its sound philosophy, the felicity of its illustrations, and the delicacy of its satire. We promise our readers a great treat from the perusal of these 'Wise Saws and Modern Instances,' which contain a world of practical wisdom, and a treasury of the richest fun."—*Post.*

VOL. VIII.—CARDINAL WISEMAN'S RECOLLECTIONS
OF THE LAST FOUR POPES.

"There is no dynasty of European sovereigns about which we English entertain so much vague curiosity, or have so little information, as about the successors to the Popedom. Cardinal Wiseman is just the author to meet this curiosity. His book is the lively record of what he has himself seen, and what none but himself, perhaps, has had so good an opportunity of thoroughly estimating. There is a gossipping, all-telling style about the book which is certain to make it popular with English readers."—*John Bull.*

"A picturesque book on Rome and its ecclesiastical sovereigns, by an eloquent Roman Catholic. Cardinal Wiseman has here treated a special subject with so much generality and geniality, that his recollections will excite no ill-feeling in those who are most conscientiously opposed to every idea of human infallibity represented in Papal domination."—*Athenæum.*

"In the description of the scenes, the ceremonies, the ecclesiastical society, the manners and habits of Sacerdotal Rome, this work is unrivalled. It is full of anecdotes. We could fill columns with amusing extracts."—*Chronicle.*

www.ingramcontent.com/pod-product-compliance
Lightning Source LLC
Chambersburg PA
CBHW031420020726
47499CB00005B/1519